Two Steps Past the Altar

Two Steps Past the Altar

PATRICIA A. BRIDEWELL

TYMM PUBLISHING LLC
COLUMBIA, SC

Paperback ISBN: 978-1-7321309-1-3
Ebook ISBN: 978-1-7321309-0-6

Publishing Assistance: Tymm Publishing LLC
Content and Copy Editing: Felicia Murrell, Jessica Barrow-Smith, Maxine Thompson
Cover and Book Design: Tywebbin Creations LLC
Photographer: Michael Clark, mclark@

michaelclarkphotographers.com

Chapter 1

Thursday Flight from Atlanta

Another rolling boom thundered in the distance, followed by a bolt of lightning that sailed past Sasha's window. Her heart plummeted as the plane dipped and swooped like a roller coaster.

Don't tell me this plane is going to crash.

She slammed the shade down with a trembling hand, releasing some of her pent-up energy. The surge of adrenaline triggered a pounding sensation in her temples. This was a bad idea. Dayle and Mike had requested an extra overnight stay for Sasha in Atlanta to pursue the Gesoff account. Both relied on their superstar sales executive to sign Wexel Pharmaceuticals' new clients, but she declined. She missed Damien and hadn't seen her man in weeks. Yes, they talked on the phone, FaceTimed or Skyped every day but seeing her fiancé's face and hearing his baritone voice was not the same as being wrapped in his arms.

Long days and late-night business dinners, mixed with adjusting to time zone changes, had finally kicked in. Sasha yawned and reclined the seat. The thunder rumbled on, and a wave of hail thumped the plane louder than a thousand tap dancers on the roof while she transitioned from head bobbing to snoozing.

A loud kaboom of a thunder crash awakened her. She jumped, gripping the armrest beside her with manicured nails. The weatherman's forecast of cloudy with scattered showers was nowhere near accurate. This was a lot more than "scattered showers."

"You okay," asked the young woman next to her.

Sasha tried to smile away her anxiety as she placed a hand over her chest. "Yes. At least I will be if this thunder and lightning ever stops."

"I know what you mean. It's my first time on a plane, and my heart is racing," the woman said.

"Lord, help us!" Another passenger's whispered prayer was loud enough to be heard throughout the cabin.

"Ladies and gentlemen, we're experiencing quite a bit of turbulence. Please fasten your seatbelts and keep them fastened until the seatbelt sign is turned off," the pilot announced over the loudspeaker.

Sasha glanced around. All the flight attendants, both male and female were strapped into their single seats near the mid and back area of the plane. She took note of their terse facial expressions. A frequent flyer with lots of sky miles, she knew this could be serious.

The lights went out all over the plane, only the beeline of lights on the floor were visible. "Oooh," someone on the plane groaned. Almost as soon as they went out, the lights flickered and came back on.

An audible sigh of relief temporarily calmed her worries.

Embarrassed, she turned to her seat mate. "As much as my job keeps me in the air, I should be over flight nerves. But every time I experience a fierce storm in the air, it's like riding on a plane for the first time all over again. And I think this might be the worst storm I've ever seen in all my years of traveling."

"I know what you mean. I should have checked the weather forecast," the woman said. "I would've postponed this trip myself. This bad weather, the plane shaking. I won't be flying again anytime soon." she said.

From her limited view, Sasha observed other passengers. A few of them appeared anxious. Some shifted in their seats, and some had their heads bowed in what looked like silent prayer.

Others appeared unbothered, their attention lost in a book or their eyes covered as they slept. How anyone could sleep through this calamity was weird. Had their fear made them immune to the possibility of dying aboard this flight? Sasha's curiosity forced her to peek behind the lowered shade at a blurry glaze coating the 747 aircraft window. Every time thunder roared, her heart beat faster.

"You said you fly a lot for work. What do you do?" The lady asked.

Sasha was grateful for the woman's question. It drew her attention away from the window. "I'm a pharmaceutical sales rep."

"Oh, wow. I'm in school for my MBA with a focus on marketing."

"Well, good for you. Where do you attend?" Sasha turned

around to see the flight attendants still seated. She twirled a piece of hair around her finger.

"Cal-State Long Beach."

Images of Damien scrolled in her head faster than a spinning top, and Sasha grinned. A go-getter, she admired his tenacity. He had achieved gunnery sergeant rank and an executive chef position in the Marines. Beyond real was his ability to squeeze in time for table tennis matches. *Incredible man!*

"My fiancé graduated from CSU Long Beach, and he holds them in high esteem. What's your plan after graduation?"

"Well, if I make it through this flight, I'd like to get into sales one day."

Sasha pulled out a business card from her handbag. "Here, keep this. When you get your degree, feel free to call me. If you want to go far in life, who you know is more important than what you know."

She noticed the excitement dancing in the woman's eyes and smiled.

"Thank you so much," the woman said as she scanned the card. "Sasha. Beautiful name. I'm Roxanne, by the way." She reached over to shake Sasha's hand.

"Nice to meet you—"

A brutal crack of blue-white lightning split the sky in half from top to bottom cutting off Sasha's words. An explosion of thunder shook the plane like an earthquake in heaven. *Surely the world is ending.*

Yet somehow, they lived on and the plane kept cruising.

Mentally exhausted over the weather conditions, she lifted the shade enough to peer through the window and closed it. She glanced at Roxanne's pale face, her skin appeared drained of color. The poor girl could almost pass for white. Not only did she notice Roxanne's deathly frightened expression, but she also looked vaguely familiar. Sasha was confident she had seen her somewhere before.

Sasha touched her arm. "Trust me, I'm scared too. When I was ten, lightning struck the pavement while I was playing outdoors."

Roxanne shook her head. "Wow. Must've been scary."

"It was. I try to stay out of lightning's way. But like I said, my job requires a lot of flying and these storms get nasty, but we always come out all right." Sasha forced a smile for Roxanne's sake. "We'll be okay."

"I hope so," Roxanne said softly.

The weather out there was no joke, and the thunder and lightning had seared every nerve in her body. But the plane soared on through the stormy sky. "So, tell me more about you. Where are you from and when do you graduate?" Sasha asked Roxanne.

The two conversed throughout most of the flight, which made the flight less traumatizing. As the plane approached Los Angeles, Sasha lifted the shade to clear skies and the warmth of a sunny California day. *What a blessing to be back home.*

Upon landing, she pulled out her cell. *Hmmm. Two texts from Damien and three voicemails from Mom.* Knowing her mom, she had probably called the airport several times for an update.

"Well, you were right. We made it out alive," Roxanne said with a smile. She grabbed a small duffle bag from the overhead bin.

"Yes, and I'm thankful. And don't forget, you have my card. Call me after you graduate," Sasha told her.

"I will and thank you for the pep talk." She waved at Sasha and walked away.

A glance over her shoulder revealed the harried expressions of passengers scrambling down the aisle. She inhaled a cleansing breath and laid her head against the seat for a moment before unfastening her seatbelt. Relieved that her seat was near the front, she lifted her bag and got in line.

Immediately after Sasha stepped off the plane, she dashed through the bustling crowd, zig-zagging in between a few stragglers. She excused herself as she passed an older woman who gave her the beady eye. She glanced back after politely maneuvering past the elderly lady just in time to see the woman give her the middle finger. Sasha laughed out loud. Rudeness was not her character, and at this point, her focus was beating the swarm at the Southwest Airlines baggage claim. She was ready to get the heck out of LAX.

Chapter 2

Los Angeles

Sasha pulled out her claim ticket and rechecked the flight number. The luggage rumbled as it fell onto the conveyor belt. She spotted her tan luggage, inspected the name tag and swung it to the floor. Pivoting, she ran into a brick wall, also known as her fiancé's chest.

"Ma'am, you need any help? Your bag seems kind of heavy," Damien said with a thick Southern drawl that only he could do so well.

"Baby!" she hollered, completely forgetting about the luggage as she folded her arms around his neck. She kissed his thick lips before hiding her face in his neck, breathing in Paul Sebastian, his favorite cologne. Sasha felt his bulky arms tighten around her waist. *God, it feels so good to be back in his arms again. Three weeks of longing and missing him felt like ages.*

"I missed you, too," he chuckled, airlifting her into a spin before carefully placing her on her feet again. "Wow, you look amazing. Did you get more beautiful while you were gone?"

"Oh, Damien, stop," she laughed, smacking his arm.

He gathered her luggage, and she followed him out of the airport. Grinning from ear to ear; Sasha couldn't take her eyes off him. Her soon-to-be husband had stepped things up a notch since she'd last seen him. He always kept his hair cut close and his moustache neatly trimmed, but his edge-up seemed even sharper. His biceps were larger, and his chest chiseled with muscles. A collared shirt could barely hold his muscular physique, and the way his jeans stretched across his thighs. *Mercy, mercy.*

"How was the flight?" He loaded her suitcase in the trunk.

"Nightmarish, to say the least." She waited for him to unlock the car. "But I met a sharp young lady on the plane. We talked each other through the storm, so that eased my anxiety. Hers, too."

Damien slid behind the wheel and leaned toward Sasha. The kiss he planted on her lips nearly lifted her out of her seat.

"You think we could make a hotel stop?" Breathless, she gave him a naughty smile.

"For what? That's wasting money."

"Something different. Ple-e-ase," she begged with pouty lips. "It's been a long time since we've sat in a hot tub together."

He chuckled and shook his head. "Nah, sweet lady. We can do the hot tub another time. Got a lot of ground to cover today and not a lot of time to play around. Work first, play later, right?"

"Okay." She crossed her arms. "What are we doing today besides meeting with the wedding planner?"

"First, your mom's getting discharged from the hospital today. Last time I checked with Bishop, she was waiting for her medications. So, we need to go check on her. Next, we meet with the wedding planner at one and the cake lady at three for the cake-tasting."

"Jeez, I thought mom was home when we talked this morning." Sasha plopped a hand against her forehead. She was hoping she'd be able to slip over to the office after their meeting with the wedding planner and a rendezvous with Damien. But it seemed like that was out of the question now.

"And, I have something special planned for us tonight."

"Something special like?"

"Homemade dinner and you for dessert."

"Mmm." She leaned her head against his shoulder, body thrumming at the thought.

"Mmm hmm." Damien agreed, lacing his fingers through hers. He pulled her hand to his lips and kissed the back of her fist.

He was right. They did have a busy day, and the hours ticked by in a blur. They went to her parents' house to check on her mother, but she was already in bed by the time they got there. Her mother's health had started deteriorating over the last several months, and her doctor was concerned with the inability to control her malignant hypertension. He had tried various medications for years and all had failed to maintain her blood pressure within normal limits. Watching her mother gradually lose interest in gardening, tutoring, and other activities was painful. Even worse was her mother's poor prognosis and risk for an early death if her physician did not find an effective medication. Sasha didn't want to bother her mother so she told her father she'd call and check on her later.

"Good timing. I think we'll get to the restaurant in time." Damien said.

"We should. If we run a little late, I'm sure Amiya will wait."

"Your dad had some pep in his voice this morning."

Sasha sighed. Thoughts of her father taking care of her mom and handling his ministry warmed her heart. "I'm sure he feels better now that Mom is home."

Damien exited the 405 Freeway and eased onto Center Drive in Culver City. The slanted palm trees and lush green landscape accompanied by the sun painted a cozy setting.

"Yes, I think he's fine now. Your father can preach, but he sure can't cook. He had me cooking for him the entire weekend while your mom was hospitalized, and he would never come straight out and ask." Damien chuckled. "He'd say, 'Son, what we eating tonight?'"

Sasha laughed and shook her head. He imitated her father's voice so well. "And you loved every minute of it."

"You know I did," he admitted with a smile. "Then, on Sunday, we had been at church half the day and visited your mom. I thought it was too late to cook, so I suggested stopping for turkey burgers. Bishop gave me that look and said, 'Son, I don't want no turkey burger.'"

Sasha laughed again. "He rarely eats out except with Mom. And they eat out on Sundays."

"Oh, I know. He told me. I gave in and whipped up a quick meal. Salmon and scallops in Alfredo sauce, roasted veggies, and brown rice. Man, Bishop ate that food like it was going out of style."

"I'm sure he did!"

"In fact, he loved it so much he wants me to start a cooking class at the church twice a month."

"What?" Sasha raised an eyebrow.

"Yes. It's a class to educate on cooking healthier meals. Our folks gotta cut out the oxtails and ham hocks. They can eat soul food without the salt and grease."

"Sounds good. What happened to the table tennis classes for teens?"

"He still wants me to do those, too."

"You live and work on the base several hours away. How can you spearhead both of those auxiliaries with your schedule?"

"Well, for one, I'm retiring early. Two, I have a beautiful wife-to-be who has my back, so I know she'll help me." He patted her thigh.

"Damien."

"Sasha." She sighed heavily. "Baby, you know how busy I am. My father already has me over the Women in Prosperity ministry, and that's time-consuming enough."

"I know, I know. You have Ebony helping, though. I'm thinking with you and a couple of volunteers, I can pull it off."

"Ebony is swamped with school, work, and raising Asia.

I'm just thankful that she's temporarily leading the WIP Ministry for me."

"We're about to get married, sweet lady. I'm hoping you'll slow your job down some. We need time for us. And don't forget our trip to Augusta. Okay?"

Sasha touched her fingers to her temple and shook her head. "Babe, I'm in Georgia all the time. I promise we'll visit your family. I just had a terrifying plane ride. Can we discuss this another time?"

"Okay, sweet lady," he said softly. "I'ma let it go this time. But, remember we need to settle this before our wedding."

Thankful for the brief reprieve, Sasha lowered her seat back and rested while Damien drove to their destination.

They met the wedding planner at Alejo's Presto Trattoria Italian Restaurant. She was a stick of a woman. Her legs were about the size of Sasha's arms, but she wore her natural hair big and bold. A multicolored scarf wrapped around a thick bushel of hair was the largest object on her body. Sasha thought she resembled a walking lollipop, but the woman was smart and could articulate well. That's why Sasha had hired her.

Amiya opened her large planner, jotting down notes. "I'd like to suggest we go ahead and determine the rehearsal dates."

Sasha glanced at Damien who shrugged.

"I think it's too soon," Sasha said. "I'd rather wait a few months before the wedding. My bridesmaids have to travel."

"Well, it's never too soon to start planning," Amiya said with a hint of snappiness. "Throw out some dates I can work into my schedule. I like to plan to avoid wasting my time. I'm sure you understand."

Damien looked at Sasha. She tapped her nails against the table but didn't answer. "We understand," he nodded, taking over. "Let's say tentatively, the Thursday before the wedding. But if we need to change, we'll let you know in advance."

"And what about the cake? Did you finalize a bakery?"

"We're actually meeting with the pastry chef today," Damien said.

"The last time we met you said you were meeting with her. What happened with that?"

"She had to reschedule." Damien bit his lower lip.

"Well, if she's giving you the run-around, maybe you should consider another pastry chef. She's not the only one in L.A. who makes cakes, you know?" Amiya pulled out her iPad and began tapping away. "I have a list right here."

"We don't need your list." Sasha was trying to keep the edge out of her voice. "She's in our budget and we like her work. There's a reason why they say patience is a virtue."

"And there's also a reason why they say why put off for tomorrow what you can do today." Amiya grinned broadly and continued to scroll through her iPad.

Sasha's cell chimed. "Excuse me," she said with a tight jaw. "I'm taking this call."

Chapter 3

Sasha took the call inside the bathroom. "Hey Tamar."

"Hey girlfriend!" Tamar squealed in the phone in her high-pitched voice. "I didn't think you would answer. I figured you were still in the air."

"No, my plane touched down hours ago." Sasha turned on her Bluetooth. "We did have two delays because of the weather. I'm just glad we landed safely. That storm was gruesome."

"Huh. You think that was gruesome? Honey, I could strangle someone right now."

Sasha rolled her eyes. "What did Xavier do this time?"

"Oh, it wasn't him. It was the florist. They got my order all wrong! I asked for a colorful mix to match the bridesmaids' dresses, and they ordered carnations. Those things break me out in hives. The Best Florist in Town is the worst. But thank God I caught it in time. They put in a rush-order, and the flowers will be here before the wedding day. You're still flying in for the final rehearsal, right?"

"You know I am."

"Good. Because one bridesmaid told me she's driving in and might be late. I swear, if Lynne wasn't a close friend I'd tell her not to come. Like she didn't know about this months ago, but don't get me started on that or I'll be on the phone all day. This wedding stuff is getting on my nerves. I'm just ready for it to be over."

"Girl, Lynne will never change. We're here meeting with our wedding planner now, and I'm telling you, if she says another cockamamie thing to me, I'm firing her little sarcastic behind."

"No, you didn't go there!" Tamar laughed so hard she made Sasha laugh too.

"Let me head back inside. I left Damien in there with Medusa and I need to go save him." A yawn stretched her mouth open as wide as Dodger Stadium.

"None of that yawning. I still have a long day ahead of me, and I don't need you making me tired."

"Girl, jetlag," Sasha sighed. "I just need a nap. A nice, long nap."

"Well, you travel a lot so you should be tired. You plan to slow down after the wedding?"

"Slow down? How many glasses of wine have you had? You know me. I'm trying to get a promotion not a demotion."

"Well, we'll see what Damien has to say about that."

"Absolutely nothing. He knows I love working."

"That's cool. Girl, Xavier told me not to even think about any traveling unless he's coming with me." Tamar laughed.

"Okay, but that's Xavier. No need to worry about Damien." Sasha checked her reflection in the mirror, tousled her curly black hair, and added another coating of almost-nude matte lipstick. "I promise you, when we get home today, I will supply *all* of my man's needs so that will be the least of his worries."

Tamar laughed. "Okay, girlfriend, I hear you. But it seems like Damien has one thing to worry about."

"What's that?"

"Not what...*who*."

"I assume you're talking about Xavier's best man."

"Mr. Wesley Dunbar hasn't stopped talking about you since he met you at the conference."

"Is that a fact?" Sasha tilted her head, thinking of the first time she met Wesley. *The tall, linebacker hunk of a man walked into the networking reception. Cute, she thought. Player. Football hero out for a one-night stand. But she wasn't too impressed so that wasn't happening. At least not with her. She watched in her periphery as he strutted across the room in her direction. The light reflected a glow on his face that she hadn't noticed upon his entrance. He flashed a dimpled-chin smile, and his boyish face caught her full attention. Wearing a snazzy charcoal gray suit, pink shirt, and a gray and pink tie, he was a walking billboard for GQ Magazine.*

"Good evening, I'm Wesley Dunbar." He extended his hand with a business card tucked between two fingers. "And you are?"

His eloquent voice made her body shiver, and she hesitated before taking his business card. Her tongue felt like a thick lump of Silly Putty clay. Yet somehow, she managed to shake his hand. "Sasha. Sasha Ed...Edmonds." Why was she so nervous? She wasn't at the conference searching for a man. In fact, if Tamar hadn't insisted she accompany her to the pharmaceutical conference, she wouldn't have attended.

"Sasha, you still there?"

She snapped out of her daydream. "Where else would I be?"

"Well, I'm asking you straight out. What's going on between you and Wes?"

"Business, and that's all I'm saying, okay?"

Tamar paused. "So, it's all innocent?"

"Girl, bye. I'll see you soon."

"Sasha, wait. Tell me this. Are you and Damien cool?"

"Of course. Look, I'm in the bathroom." She furrowed her brow, surveying the bathroom to make sure no one had walked in. "We're in the middle of planning our wedding, so why the questions?"

"Forget it."

"No, really. I want to know."

"You know...after Jared—"

"Jared? He's history, and didn't I say not to mention him again? Damien is my prince and I love him."

"Okay. You're upset. Let's end this talk."

"Whatever, Tamar. I'll see you soon."

She took a deep, steady breath. Sometimes Tamar went way overboard on their friendship. She didn't need to sort through every single detail of Sasha's life to rearrange or fix it. Truth be told, Tamar had hit a few walls in her dating life while at Spelman, as did Carleen and Elaine. And Lynne? She wouldn't attempt to count the number of snags she'd had with men in college. To dwell on a post college heartthrob who massacred their savory love-life didn't make sense. *Controlling, deceitful, cheating, crazy man.* That was Jared. She left him so she wouldn't go crazy. That period of her life was like the end of a slow fall after diving off a skyscraper. She had learned to be a better judge of a man's character.

Yes, Wesley was attracted to her, and there was nothing wrong with that. Like she'd said, their relationship was all about business—and the medication for her mother.

Sasha walked back into the restaurant; Amiya was gone. She didn't realize she was holding her breath until she exhaled, and her shoulders dropped.

"Our cake lady just canceled on us again," Damien held up his cell phone. "Maybe Amiya is right. Perhaps we should consider another baker for a backup plan."

Sasha shrugged. "That's fine. Let's go. I'm ready to go home."

"But our food."

"It can wait."

"Baby, we've already ordered."

She leaned close and put her lips against his ear, allowing him to feel the heat of her breath against his skin before sucking gently on his earlobe. "Babe, I'm ready to go home. The food can wait."

Not hesitating any longer, Damien stood. "Yeah, sweet lady, I believe you're right." He hooked his arm through hers and tossed two twenty-dollar bills on the table. "We can always eat later."

Grinning, they speed-walked out of the restaurant, and

Damien broke a few speed limits to make it home faster. As they approached her street, she sighed. Ten years had sailed by faster than a speedboat. It seemed like yesterday when her realtor called to inform her that the loan for her property had been approved. The pride on her face brightened her parents' living room when she mentioned the cute two-bedroom townhouse in the View Park-Windsor Hills District of Los Angeles. Moving to a larger home with Damien would be hard because she loved her place but deciding to have a baby would be harder. At thirty-six years-old, she still wasn't ready, and Damien couldn't wait to be a father.

Damien pulled in the back to the carport.

"Let's see who gets inside first," he said, exiting the car.

"Uh huh, you cheater. You know I have to get my bag and computer."

"Yep, see you inside." Laughing, he did a light jog down the driveway.

A few minutes later, she walked inside. The flow of running water from the shower signaled that Damien was ready for playtime. He took her computer and purse and laid them on the couch before clamping her in a bearhug.

He tipped her chin upward. "Sweet Lady, I love you so much."

"I know, babe. I love you, too." With bodies pressed together, they lingered in a deep kiss. His warm lips against hers set off a skyrocket of emotions. She had missed his hands roaming her body in all the right places.

At times, she had doubts about marriage. Could she

transition to a Molly Homemaker type of woman and still work? Would she fall prey to Damien's dreams and wind up barefoot and pregnant with a house full of kids? She dismissed her wedding day jitters and focused on the positive aspects of married life like coming home to her man every day.

"Honey, the shower." Sasha broke the kiss.

"Well, let's get going before we flood the place," he said, unbuttoning her blouse.

They finished undressing in the bathroom. Tops flew one way, bottoms another. They couldn't seem to reach the shower fast enough, almost falling over kicked-off shoes. Damien pushed the shower door open, and she stepped into the fragrance of Lavender Rain body wash. He used his chiseled chest to back her against the cool tile, kissing her long and hard. His hands caressed her breasts while he planted tender kisses on her neck. He worked his way back down to her breasts, his tongue circling her nipples while his long fingers explored her genitals. She moaned. *If only this could last forever.* Lifting her hips to his waist, Sasha wrapped her legs around his body as they became one. She lost herself inside Damien's sweet lovemaking — and work, emails, wedding plans, even her doubts, lost their importance in the moment. It all had to wait.

Chapter 4

Early the next morning, Sasha woke with a tingling bladder demanding to be relieved. Groggy and a bit sore from three long nights of lovemaking, she almost fell out the bed trying to stand on her wobbly legs. Damien had an insatiable hunger for sex. It didn't matter how many rounds they had, in ten minutes or so, he was standing at full attention ready to go again. She glanced at his empty side of the bed. Where was Mr. King of Making Love this morning?

Sasha emptied her bladder, pumped soap into her hands and washed them before walking to the living room. No Damien. "Babe, you in the kitchen?" Maybe he'd gone to the store. He most likely couldn't find what he needed to fix breakfast since she rarely cooked. She walked back to the bedroom, threw on her robe, brushed her teeth then headed towards the kitchen.

A folded card sat on the table alongside a dome-covered platter. She unfolded the card.

Every day and night with you was indescribable. Had to leave early to return to base. Sorry I couldn't stay for church. I'll be home hopefully the day before you fly out for Tamar's wedding. Love you, sweet lady.

"Aww. I love you too, Damien. Now I have to tell Dad you won't be in church." Sasha lifted the dome. The aroma wafting from the plate added fragrance to the room. A career as a chef was the perfect fit for Damien because the man loved to cook. He'd made her ham and cheese crepes with some type of creamy sauce drizzled over top and homemade hash potatoes. The plate was still a little warm. She grinned. Thankfully, he didn't leave with the funky attitude he had the night before.

In and out of sleep while he was in the bathroom showering, through partially closed lids she watched him saunter across the room in his entire naked splendor. She faked a light snooze.

"Wake up, sleepy head." He planted a kiss against her forehead. "I know you're not asleep." Damien nibbled on her earlobe and slid his hand under her gown.

"All, right, lover boy. What's up with the fifty giddy-ups? This gal is whipped."

"What are you saying, Sasha?" His forehead crinkled.

"I'm saying... Aren't you tired, babe? You've been riding me nonstop...for hours."

"Aww, come on. For hours? That's not true, and I didn't hear you complaining."

"Honestly, it was awesome. But I'm tired. For a moment, I thought you'd taken Viagra or something."

She laughed, but Damien twisted his mouth. "Man, I try to make love to my woman and this is what I get. We haven't made love in... I can't even remember."

He snatched his pajamas off the chair and put them on. "Now really, do I need Viagra?"

Sasha folded her arms. "Well, you don't have to get so pissy. I was just joking."

"That wasn't a good joke," He glared at her before walking off. "I'm making a sandwich."

It wasn't like Damien to get upset so easily. Sure, he was a great lover, and she didn't mean to insult him. But she'd had enough loving to last a decade. After tossing back and forth for a while, she knew what she had to do. It wouldn't have been right to sleep while her honey fumed over an insensitive comment. She'd walked into a dark living room and found Damien wrapped in a blanket on the couch, snoring. She kissed his forehead and went back to bed.

Sasha placed the card back on the table. He could have told her he was leaving. This situation was getting downright silly. Every time she was home, he was stuck on base. Every time he was home, she was flying to Atlanta or wherever her job sent her. Maybe Tamar was right. Maybe she did need to slow things down at her job. How else would their marriage survive if neither of them was ever here? At the same time, Sasha couldn't see herself going backward at work, not when she'd struggled to make it to where she was now.

Countless years of working a mid-level position in the pharmaceutical field had finally allowed her an opportunity to climb the ladder of success. She was a key on the middle ring but still trying to make it to the top. The position she was up for at Wexel would be that final climb, complete with a huge salary increase and a plethora of autonomy. Plus, she would delegate the workload evenly among the sales team like the rest of the corporateers did at Wexel.

Sasha ate every bite of the rich, delicious food then walked to the bathroom to shower. She savored the feel of the hot water, raining down and massaging her sore muscles, until it ran cold then wrapped herself in a towel. An unfamiliar ringtone lured her into her bedroom. Interest piqued, she knotted the towel around her breasts, searching for the jazz tune.

She dropped to her knees and raised the bedspread. A bluish light glowed from a cell phone screen that read: Friend.

Before the phone could stop ringing, Sasha grabbed it. "Hello?"

The caller didn't reply, but she could hear breathing.

"Hello," Sasha said a little louder.

"Ooops. Ummm, wrong number," the female voice said, quickly disconnecting.

Sasha sat on the side of the bed and stared at the phone. *Wonder who that was?* Wrong numbers find their way to everybody's phones at some point. She walked in the direction of the bathroom then paused. Torn about whether to call back or forget it, she threw up her hands. *What the heck? I need to see who called my man.* She dialed and waited, but there was no answer. Her mind started wandering to places it shouldn't. Damien had never given her any reason to believe he was unfaithful.

She finished dressing just as her phone rang.

"Hello, Kitten. Is Damien around?"

"Hey, Dad, Damien rushed out of here before I got up."

"Aww, no. I thought he might've come by and cooked breakfast before church."

"Uh, yes, he did that," Sasha knew full well if her dad knew what else he'd done, he would faint. And then, he'd have them come in for counseling and prayer.

"I was hoping to see you two in church."

"I know. Unfortunately, we won't be there. I have some work to finish."

"I hate to hear that. Can you try him at the base later?"

"He left his cell here."

She could call his department on base but getting him on the line always took forever. She had to go through so many people before they transferred her call to his line, and even then, she only got him if he was in the office, which was hardly ever.

She sighed. "I can try, Dad. What's up?"

"Let him know I already have three young women and two males interested in the cooking classes. The guys are fresh off the streets, high-school dropouts. They're interested and want a start date. So, I need a tentative date from Damien."

"Wow, that's awesome. I'll let him know. How's Mom?"

"Still recuperating."

"Is she feeling better?"

"Well, as best as can be expected. She's been sleeping a lot; her pressure is not where it should be. I just thank God she's home."

"Did she take her meds this morning?"

"Yeah, the same medicine she's been taking."

"That medicine is obviously not working if she landed in the ER again."

"Honey, calm your voice. She has a follow-up appointment with her doctor Tuesday and I'm sure they'll get that taken care of."

"Can you at least talk to her about considering—"

"Sasha, stop. I'm not gonna have this conversation with you. I called to speak to Damien. Your mother is an intelligent, competent woman of God. If the medicine won't carry her through, she knows a Man who will. Sometimes, you have to rely on faith and not facts."

"I understand that, Dad, but God also gives us common sense and—"

"I'm not listening to this foolishness."

"Yeah, and maybe that's the problem. Maybe the reason why my phone doesn't ring often with you on the other end is because you're always too busy tracking down Damien."

"What's gotten into you? It's like you want to fight with me. First about your mom's health, now about phone calls. Is everything okay?"

"No, everything's not okay." But when her father got in this kind of mindset, talking to him was not going to change anything. He'd only see it from his perspective, giving little or no credence to her concerns. He knew she was up for a promotion at Wexel, and not once had he asked her how the promotion was going or whether she'd landed the position. Nothing. But she'd lost count of how many times he'd asked her about a Women in Prosperity meeting. He stayed on her about that. If it was about church, she had his full attention.

If it was about her personally, that didn't matter much to him. She didn't know why it still bothered her. He had been this way her whole life. Maybe he had wanted a son, and Damien was the son he never had. Why she expected him to change now was beyond her.

Chapter 5

Sasha ended the call with her father and did what she always did when life became a bit stressful—work. She wrote up a few reports, responded to some emails, and then prepared notes for her upcoming sales presentation.

Unfortunately, Damien's phone kept ringing the whole day with various individuals trying to reach him. That's when the idea came to surprise him on base. He wouldn't be back for a while so why not take the two-hour drive and deliver his phone? Maybe they could go out to dinner.

As she drove to Camp Pendleton, Sasha's phone lit up with a text message from Wesley Dunbar, which instantly made her smile. She had texted him earlier, asking for an update on the drug Maxitensin, which would help regulate her mother's blood pressure and get her out of the red with her health. Anxious, she opened the text and read it. *Hi, Sweetheart. Hope your day is as lovely as you. Sadly, there are no new updates. The results of the clinical trials remain consistent, which was a positive thing, and the study group will be open to new participants soon. Looking forward to seeing your lovely face when you're in town for the wedding. Save some time for me.* Soon. What was soon? But her hopes were deflated once again.

She needed something more definitive than that. *Soon* gave her zero peace of mind. *Soon* didn't make her feel any more confident about her mother's health than she felt earlier while talking on the phone with her dad. Sighing, she used the Google talk-to-text feature and texted back, "Thanks for the update."

She tossed her phone on the passenger seat and continued cruising down the 5 South Freeway. Her thoughts returned to Damien, and she grinned thinking about the last three nights. The lovemaking had been sensual, gentle and sweet. He was ready to make her his wife, and she was ready for him to be her husband. Even after being with him for the last three days, she still wanted to taste her honey's full lips and fall into his muscular embrace.

Her cell phone rang with a number she didn't recognize.

"Hello?"

"Sweet lady."

She grinned. "Hey, love."

"Listen, uh... I can't seem to find my phone."

"I got it. It fell under the bed."

He heaved a sigh of relief. "Man, I'm so glad to hear that. I thought I left it on the back of my car when I drove off. Can I ask a favor?"

"What's that?"

"You think maybe you can mail it to me, overnight mail? I won't have time to drive back home."

She thought about telling him that she was on her way to San Diego but decided to go with her plan of surprising him. "Sure, babe, I can do that. You still at work?"

"Nope, I'm at the gym now. Gonna work this body out some and head back to the base."

"You have plans tonight?"

"Uh... What makes you ask?"

"No reason. Just curious."

"Nah...no plans," he said after a few seconds more of hesitation.

"Okay, well, I'll let you get back to the gym. Love you. Talk to you later."

"Love you too, sweet lady."

After exiting the freeway, she pulled into the gym parking lot and grinned broadly when she spotted Damien's gray Jeep Grand Cherokee. He'd promised himself a new truck after he retired. Sasha figured after serving in the military for almost twenty years and driving the same truck for eight of those, he deserved something new. She flipped the overhead mirror down, turned her head from side-to-side, and pinned her hair up. Before spritzing her neck with her favorite fragrance that had hints of vanilla and lavender, she applied lip gloss then headed inside.

She strolled the long aisles, checking out the rows of exercise equipment and the people working out and engaging with others. She spotted Damien and a half-moon slid across her lips. He wore gray sweats and a black body shirt that sculpted his hairy chest and swollen arms. An attractive slender woman summoned him with her index finger and a grin.

Sasha assumed the woman was an employee, but within minutes, she eliminated that opinion. Damien walked too close to the woman, invading her personal space. Sasha watched the woman put her lips to Damien's ear and whisper something, her body pressing into his until they were aligned. Glued together with their sweat. Sasha squinted. *What?* She tilted her head and pressed her hands onto her hips. *Oh, no, this can't be happening.* A shudder ran through her before a dull ache slammed the pit of her stomach. She froze in place.

Damien was laughing as he touched the small of the woman's back. He whispered something in her ear, which sent them both into cahoots. He positioned himself behind her; her gigantic booty pressed against the front crotch area of his jogging pants as he held her arms up in the air. They lowered into a squat together; their bodies in one of the most provocative positions Sasha had ever seen. It was all she needed to see.

Hands still on her hips, she stomped over to where they stood.

"So, this is what you do while I'm away?" She said to Damien through clenched teeth.

The shock of seeing her was apparent as he stood and made space between himself and the woman. "Sasha! Baby, what are you doing here?"

"What am I doing here? I'm your *fiancé*. I came up here to surprise you, but I guess the joke's on me, huh?" She pointed at the woman who glared at Damien. "Who are you and how long have you been screwing my fiancé?"

"Screwing your fiancé?" The woman stepped forward with a scowl, but Damien stepped in between them.

He held up his hands. "Sasha, you got this all wrong. Let's go outside and talk."

"Day, what's going on?" The other woman asked him, looking confused.

"You know what?" Sasha shook her head. "I don't want to talk to you about nothing. Talk to her." She threw his cell phone at him and he caught it.

Eyes blurred by hot tears, she started walking toward the door as fast as her legs would carry her. Why had she decided to do this? She should've known the storm on the plane was a bad omen. Never in a million years had she expected this would be waiting on her at the gym. Maybe she should've just express mailed the phone like he requested. But then, she would've missed this, and she needed to see this. She thought Damien was different, that he was above these games, this shallowness.

"Sasha, wait." She turned to see him running after her. "Hey, give me a chance to explain."

She exited the gym, and her fast walk turned into a run as she attempted to get to her car. In her haste, she bumped into a few people but didn't stop to apologize. The ball of emotions caught in her throat wouldn't allow her to form words. What did she have to say to Damien anyway? It was clear he had another woman. The way they touched. The way they laughed. The way their bodies moved together as though they were one. There was way too much intimacy between them, like this had been going on for a while. And she called him Day? A pet-name? An endearment? Oh, God. How had she missed the signs? Living apart from each other hadn't been easy, but she should've known better. She just assumed that maybe she'd met one man that truly loved her.

She stopped at her car and dug in her purse for her keys but couldn't find them.

Breathless and sweaty, Damien caught up to her. He wiped the sweat from his face with a towel. "Why didn't you tell me you were on the way?"

"Why, so I wouldn't catch you doing this?"

"Catch me doing what?"

She hit his brick-hard bicep with her balled fist, certain her balled fist was injured more than his bicep. "Don't you dare fix your mouth to say catch you doing what, like you weren't doing anything wrong."

He sighed heavily. "I know what it looked like, but it's not true."

Sasha found her keys and opened her car. She threw her purse on the seat. "What's not true? That I didn't see you in there feeling on another woman with my own two eyes?"

"She's a friend. I'm just her trainer. That's it."

"Oh, really?" Sasha folded her arms and shifted her weight. "So, you touch all your trainees like that?"

"Baby—"

She held up a hand to stop him. "You're in the Marines. You play professional table tennis. And now Damien, who is always so busy, suddenly has time to train her, too? Ple-e-ase."

"Forget all that. Let's go for coffee and talk." He took several steps toward her and she cringed. If he touched her, she would go to jail for assault today. She was holding her composure by nothing more than a thread. A single thread. And he was really testing it.

"Don't even try it," she said, extending a palm. "You just made me look like a fool, and now you want coffee? The engagement is off." She twisted her engagement ring from her finger and threw it at Damien. He tried to catch the ring as it bounced off his chest and fell to the ground.

He picked up the ring. "I can't believe you're doing this. You're breaking up with me 'cause you saw me training a friend? That's irrational."

"Don't you dare call me irrational!" She stomped her foot and swung her fist in the air. "What's irrational is you thinking I'm irrational. That's what men do. They mess up, and then turn it on you, like somehow you're the crazy one. But I'm not crazy." She was thirty-six years old, and the same thing she said she'd never let happen again had slipped up on her. Another cheating, lying man. After her breakup nine years ago with Jared, she said never again. She didn't walk down the aisle to him, and she sure wouldn't walk the aisle for Damien either.

She leaned against her car and sucked in a deep breath to regain her composure. "I saw everything. And boy were you feeling the gusto. Moving your hands all over her sleazy body. You were practically dry humping her in public. I bet you're sleeping together too, right?"

Damien glanced around. A small audience had gathered, listening to their private conversation. He wiped away droplets of sweat from his forehead. "Can we talk in the car?"

"Wow, you can't even answer the question," Sasha's voice trembled, but she refused to cry in front of him. "How many times? Is it just her or are there others? You might as well be honest because it's all out of the bag now."

He chewed his lower lip and caught Sasha's gaze. "I'm not discussing this out here. For once, would you just listen to me? You're wrong about this. Come on, let's get outta here and go talk."

Sasha got in her car and started the engine. She glanced at him with a blank face. "No. I'm done talking. Go talk to her. I need your keys to my place, now."

"Sasha."

"You think I'm playing with you? I'm not. Give me the keys."

"I don't have them with me. Sasha—"

"Bring them to me this week. Ask for a day off and come pick up your stuff," she avoided his gaze. "Text me before you come and don't tell my parents about this."

Before he could speak another word, she pushed her foot to the pedal and screeched out of the parking space. She looked in her rearview mirror. Damien stood still as a statue, watching her drive away.

Tears drenched her face, dripping onto her chest, and the salt burned her skin. Nothing could eradicate the hurt and humiliation of what she saw. Nearly every man she'd dated had cheated, including that lowdown Jared. She thought Damien was different. He was raised right. He respected women. More importantly, he loved God. Her parents adored him and so did she. Why did he ruin everything?

Their wedding was three months away. And how, in God's name, would she break the news to her father who saw him more like a son than a son-in-law?

She drove for miles to make sure he hadn't followed her then turned down an isolated street and parked under a tree. She couldn't head home now. Her anxiety was too high to drive the freeway in traffic, and she felt like such a fool for being so naïve. How could he make love to her like that one night, and the next day use those same hands that had touched her body to touch some other woman's? What was so wrong with her that a man couldn't be faithful, couldn't see her worth and remain committed? Where did she miss the signs, and why did she keep getting them all wrong?

She leaned her forehead against the steering wheel and let the tears stream.

Chapter 6

Saturday

Nearly a week had passed since the run-in with Damien and his girl. Each day dragged by, and sleep had been almost nonexistent with an occasional doze here and there. After the first day or two, she had almost given in and forgiven him until her woman's intuition told her to investigate and see what else she could find. It didn't take a genius to crack his email password. That was a whole different nightmare.

Sasha rolled over in bed and stared at the alarm clock. 5:17. *Too early to get up.* Three and a half hours of sleep wasn't enough, but she couldn't force sleep despite the fatigue. She propped up on her elbows, searching for her robe that had fallen to the floor. She donned it and went into the kitchen for tea.

Hot tea in hand, she marched to her office and opened Damien's profiles for almost every dating site out there. She seethed in misery as she clicked on several different women, torturing herself with the need to review these sites again. Necessary validation for not changing her mind about calling off the wedding. She pushed her palm against her face and sipped tea while studying Honeydrop, who couldn't seem to stop sending Damien pornographic pictures of her silicone-enhanced breasts and rear-end that was wide enough to be a separate planet. Seeing the photos in his email was like splashing alcohol on an open wound.

Unable to bear the pain any longer, she shut the site down, buried her face in both hands and sobbed uncontrollably. This hurt so bad, and she had no one to confide in. Not her father or her mother. They considered Damien an angel that had found his way out of heaven. And the embarrassment of breaking this travesty to Tamar and her other friends was unimaginable. How could she tell her best friend her wedding plans were destroyed, yet keep a smile in place and be happy for Tamar's good tidings? She didn't want to be bitter, so she'd hold it all inside until she could sort things out and deal with the pain. But suffering in silence was hard.

As if dealing with Damien wasn't enough torture, her mom's blood pressure had risen to the point where they had to rush her back to the ER again. Fortunately, the doctors were able to get her blood pressure down and maintain it at an acceptable level, but they wanted to run more tests to determine why her blood pressure kept spiking.

Her mother wasn't going to die. Sasha would make sure of it, even if it meant she had to go behind her mother's back to pull a few strings. She flipped the light switch off and went back to bed.

Sasha held the phone against her ear, stirring the chicken noodle soup in her red Crock-Pot. She sniffed the aroma and returned the lid, tapping her fingers against the granite countertop as she waited. Cheesy elevator music swelled in her ear. Ten seconds, twenty seconds, thirty seconds, forty seconds. How long would they keep her on hold?

"Sorry for your wait. How can I help you?"

Really? Out of all the nurses at the facility, the lovely Debbie, Dr. Matthew's nurse, had to pick up her call. She could pick the woman's nasally voice out of a lineup.

Sasha blew air into the phone. "Can I just speak to Dr. Matthews, please?"

An equally irritated sigh and a short pause came from the other end of the phone. "He's not in the office yet. I can transfer you to his voicemail if you'd—"

"No, I don't want his voicemail. I want to speak with him. I've been calling for days, and he hasn't returned any of my calls."

"I understand your frustration. It's just. . .well, the office has been busy lately."

"I'll call later." Sasha clenched her teeth, hung up the cordless phone, and walked toward the wood-burning fireplace in her living room. She watched the orange and blue flames sway back and forth to the cadence of Mozart's masterpiece, *The Marriage of Figaro*, which played softly from a Bluetooth speaker resting on the coffee table. She rotated her shoulders to the music. The smell of burning wood elicited calmness, and she absorbed a moment of peace.

Her eyes drifted above the mantle to the portrait of her parents hugging in an endearing pose, her mother smiling into the bishop's eyes. The splendor of their purple and black formal wear, her mom's salt-and-pepper curls crowning her head, and her father's low-cut silver hair were the only indicators of their ages. Thirty-nine years of marriage and they'd survived it all. The positive, negative, and everything in between. And now that they were at the "through sickness and health" part, Mom would have to survive this too. She had too much to live for despite her poor prognosis.

She sighed again. How she wished her mother would at least consider getting a second opinion. Why she was so hellbent on only allowing Dr. Matthews to provide her care was puzzling to Sasha. If she could sit down and speak with Dr. Matthews one-on-one and share some facts and figures, maybe he would consider another treatment plan. She thought about how frail her mother looked the last time she and her father had brought her home from the hospital. It only set fire to Sasha's need to find a better solution and find one fast. Her mother had been hospitalized three times in the past year because of a bullheaded physician who must have purchased his medical license from a bootlegger.

And if that wasn't bad enough, Sasha still had to deal with Damien, who had yet to bring her house key and kept insisting they discuss the issue before making any rash decisions.

Rash decisions? No, they were more like common sense decisions. The only bad decision she could make would be to continue a relationship with him knowing who he really was.

Sasha looked down at the empty spot on her finger where her engagement ring used to be then brushed her shoulder-length curls away from her face. She didn't know how her mother did it. During her father's earlier years in the ministry, he put her mother through hell with the cheating and lies. Even as time passed, he still struggled with the spirit of infidelity. Sasha remembered as a young girl being able to pinpoint women in the church who'd had special relationships with her father. One church sister after another church sister, and more, always seemed to be in dire need of the pastor's consolations and prayers. And if Sasha could easily spot the women he'd slept with, of course her mother had to know what was going on. But her mother had turned a blind eye to her father's ways. "God is in control," she would always tell Sasha. "I'll let the Lord handle it."

And then to add insult to a healing wound, a year before Sasha went off to Spelman, a big scandal hit the community when a member accused Bishop of having an affair with the choir director. Chirps among the congregation got louder when they heard he'd purchased a new condo for her that was minutes away from the church. That was nearly two decades ago. After that huge blow-up, the mistress seemed to vanish into outer space. Bishop was asked to step down from the pulpit until the controversy diminished. With just her mother's teacher's salary paying all the bills and mortgage, Sasha watched her parents struggle to keep their home and sanity. Scholarships and picking up a night-shift job had contributed to household expenses and kept her in school when her parents could no longer afford her education. A year later, the church reinstated her father. It humbled him to a place of pure repentance, and God rebuilt and restored her family from ground zero. Through it all, Sasha's mom stayed by Bishop's side and remained committed to her vows, keeping her faith rooted and grounded in God.

Well, kudos to her. Sasha had faith, but she also had common sense, and she refused to relive that drama in a marriage. She was thirty-six—too old and too tired to be dealing with those types of games.

A swoosh of rain pummeled an open window in the living room, breaking her reverie. She closed out the whistle of gusty winds and showers and ran to the linen closet for a towel to soak up the water.

"Of all days, this is the worst for a rainstorm." She warmed her cold palms near the flames of the fireplace. The phone rang. Half hoping it was Dr. Matthews, she grabbed the phone off the coffee table and sighed when she looked at the caller ID.

"Hey, Mom," Sasha walked into the kitchen to check on the chicken noodle soup. "Soup is almost done, then I'm heading your way, okay?"

"Oh, honey, don't worry about it. The weather's too messy out there."

"I've been cooking for hours." Sasha frowned and switched her cell to speaker phone so she could stir the soup. "A little rain doesn't scare me. If thunder or lightning hits, I'm not leaving."

"Well, it scares me. Didn't you hear that thunder and rain

earlier? I tried to get Bishop to stay home. Huh. He acted like it would kill him to miss a day from church. Now he's bugging me every hour."

"That's my father for you. You know he loves his church. And no, I didn't hear any thunder, or I wouldn't be going anywhere. So, how are you feeling today?" Sasha placed six pieces of turkey bacon in a cast-iron skillet. Once it was done, she would crumble it over the soup then ladle some in a Tupperware bowl. Whether her mother liked it or not, she was bringing her parents dinner tonight, just like she'd planned.

"Tired. My blood pressure is okay, and I had some oatmeal and coffee for breakfast. Bishop made us chicken salad sandwiches for lunch and I ate that too. So, I'll feel better soon."

She sounded okay, much better than she had a few days ago. Her voice had more strength, more life in it. Almost like her old self again, albeit a bit winded.

"Well, I'm glad your appetite's back." She turned the burner down and flipped the bacon. "You really should let me bring this soup. I have to stop by Ebony's anyway and pick up my dress, so I'll be close by."

"Your wedding dress?"

"No, my bridesmaid dress for Tamar's wedding."

"Oh, when you flying out?"

"Thursday morning."

"Humph. Try to stay put for a while after you get back. If you keep traveling the way you do, you won't have a wedding like Tamar's."

Right, a wedding like Tamar's. A wedding that would never happen. Damien – her sweet, handsome, loving Damien – was now a part of her past. Wiping tears from the corners of her eyes, she tried to swallow the lump in her throat.

"How is Damien?"

Sasha hesitated. She hated hiding information from her parents, but she couldn't tell them. Not right now. "He's, uh...he's fine. He'll be back home in a few days."

"So, by the time he gets in, you'll be leaving out?" She could hear the irritation in her mother's voice. "With him always on base and you always up in the air, I don't know how you two plan to stay married."

"Yeah, I know, but we'll work it out," Sasha said softly.

Her mother cleared her throat. "Honey, listen. I know the wedding is a few months away. But are you all thinking of starting a family soon? You'll be forty in a few years."

"Mom, we've already had this conversation a thousand times—"

"No, no. I just want you to hear me out."

Sasha pursed her lips as she put out the fire in the living room and grabbed her trench coat, cinching the belt at her waist. As her mother talked, she placed her Bluetooth in her ear and headed outside to load the Tupperware bowls into the car.

"The fact that I'm still living and breathing is nothing but a miracle," her mother said. "I thought that was the end for me. And I don't know how much time I have left here on this earth—"

"Don't talk like that."

"Hush, chile, just hear me out. I don't know how much time the good Lord is going to give me on this earth. But what I do know is I don't want to leave here without having at least touched my grandchild, held him or her in my arms. I want to live to see my legacy continue through you." Her mother hesitated, sounding as though she was searching for the right words to say. "What is it, Sasha? You don't want to have kids? I never hear you talk about kids. You can be honest with me."

The rain had let up substantially, but the wind threatened to blow her back into the house as she made her way to her trunk, carefully hopping over puddles. "It's not that I don't want children or can't have them. It's...just...timing, Mom. Timing is everything."

"Well, you don't have much *time* left, dear."

"Damien and I aren't married yet. So why are we talking babies without a marriage license? And besides, with my career—"

"There's more to life than a career, Sasha. After the wedding, take some time off and ask Damien to do the same. Believe me when I say, you'll need it. I've noticed strain between you and Damien lately, and I'm sure you flying here and flying there all the time isn't helping the situation."

Ready to leave this subject, Sasha said, "I'm in the car, and I want to get off the phone so I can focus on the road if that's okay with you."

"Okay, honey. I'll see you when you get here." Her mother sounded disappointed.

Sasha sent Ebony a quick text to let her know she was on the way to pick up her gown, then turned off the radio and listened to the beating rain and the swishing wipers as they drowned out the angst and worry that raged and stormed. A bundle of conflicting emotions tangled inside her head. She gazed at the cloudy, gray sky looming over the city, praying silently that the thunder in her life would hush and the lightning would dim and cease.

Chapter 7

Saturday

As Sasha pulled along the curb and parked, she glanced at her mother smiling and waving from a lawn chair on the porch. Sasha returned the gesture, but inwardly, she cringed. Although the rain had dwindled to a misty breeze, it was still cool, and her mom should be in the house. But the porch was her favorite spot when she wasn't gardening or cooking. It didn't matter if it was icy or scorching, her mother loved being outdoors.

She got out the car and clicked the alarm then started up the driveway. Stopping in her tracks, she tapped her palm against her forehead.

"I said to myself that girl forgot the chicken noodle soup," her mother said. "What, you left it at home?"

"No, it's in the trunk. Here, Mom." Sasha walked the few short steps to the porch and handed her mother her purse. "Do you mind taking this in the house for me?"

She walked back to the car and grabbed the dress. On the seat was a yellow tablet with a list of wedding cancelations she'd checked off thus far: venue, cake decorator, photographer. She still needed to cancel the caterer and the rental company, and there were loads of wedding decorations ordered online that she would need to ship back.

"Hon, let me help you." Her mom had worked her way over to the car and was standing behind Sasha with the purse on her shoulder, one hand resting on her hip.

"Uh... Mom, I've got this. It's cool out here. Go back inside." Sasha leaned down and flipped the tablet over. Letters from Damien she had ripped up fell to the floor. She threw a sweater over the letters. *Bless her soul. My mom is a sweetie pie, but she's too nosy for her own good.*

"Girl, what you doing? Get that stuff and let's get outta this cold air."

"I've been telling you to go in the house. But no-o-o, you wanted to help." She closed the car door and opened the trunk. "Here, you can take the gown." She laid the bagged gown over her mom's arm and kissed her cheek. Her gaze drifted to her mother's sweet olive-brown face. "Always trying to help. Now go on in the house. I'll get the soup."

Sasha grabbed the Tupperware bowls from her trunk, thankful her mom hadn't noticed the tablet and envelopes. She walked into the kitchen and set the bowls on the counter before retrieving a bottle of water from the refrigerator. She glanced at the kitchen table and sighed, the red box filled with numerous medications sat in its usual spot. Her spirit dampened. Talking to her mother about a new doctor would get her nothing but an argument and a headache, so she decided to keep her comments to herself.

Her mother strolled into the room clapping her hands. "Ebony did a fine job on that gown. I love it!"

"I told you she has talent. I don't know how she gets everything done. I mean, handling an eight-year-old, school, and a job, I'd lose my mind." Sasha took a seat in a cushioned dining room chair and unscrewed the water bottle.

"No, you wouldn't. You don't have kids, but I'll tell you what. You do just as much with that demanding job of yours." Her mom shook her head and peered over her eyeglass rim. "And she's making your wedding dress too, right?"

"Yeah, she is." Sasha's eyes swept around the living room. "Did you change the curtains?"

"Bishop bought new ones while I was in the hospital. It was the first thing I noticed when I got home. They look nice, don't they? Lets more light in this place." Her mother pulled up a chair and returned her attention to Sasha. "So, how's little Asia doing? I heard she was sick."

"She had a stomach flu, but she's better. Ebony said to tell you hi and she's lifting you in prayer. They'll be back in church next week. She's still going to lead the Women in Prosperity ministry a while longer."

"That's wonderful. How'd you convince her to do it?"

"It actually didn't take much convincing. I asked her, and she jumped at the chance."

Her mother smiled. "That girl has grown so much. Young women can learn a lot from her life story and the way she's matured. I hope Bishop puts her to work more often in the church.

"Well, I wouldn't push for more work in the church. You know she's finishing her Fashion Design Degree."

Her mother threw up her hands. "Oh, I'd completely forgotten she's in school." She wiggled her nose then clapped her hands. "Honey, you got that soup smelling right! You know Bishop loves your soup. He's gonna have a fit when he comes home."

Her mother walked to the drawer and pulled out a giant spoon then stirred the soup. She looked over her shoulder.

"So how does the dress fit?"

Sasha grinned. "Perfect."

"Why don't you try it on? I want to see how it looks on you."

"Sure." Sasha stood. "Where'd you put it?"

"It's on the door in your room."

Sasha headed down the hallway, opened the door to her old bedroom and glanced around. She sat on the side of the canopy bed, picked up the pillows and hugged them. They smelled like Tide. Her mother had kept the room arranged the same way it had been before she left home years ago. It was hard to believe the same pictures of herself, friends, and favorite entertainers were still hanging on all the walls. Her eyes roamed the room and settled on the lavender and magenta gown that hung on the closet door. She removed her pullover sweater and pants and put the gown on. As she stood in the mirror, admiring how well the dress complimented her figure, she paused. *Dad.*

She rushed out the room, holding up the bottom of her dress so she wouldn't trip as she made her way into the living room. Sasha whirled around. "You like my dress?"

"It looks nice," he said, walking right past her.

Sasha tilted her head. "What's wrong, Dad?" He frowned and mumbled under his breath before opening the refrigerator. From the expression on his face something must have happened.

"Hi, hon," her mother said. "When'd you get in town?"

Sasha turned and saw her mother hugging Damien.

"This morning," Damien said, peering at Sasha beneath a raised brow as he sat in a corner chair in the living room.

Sasha squinted at him and moved her attention back to her father in the kitchen. Her dad's behavior made sense now. Damien had told him. Why else would her dad be acting so strange? She glared at Damien, who slightly shrugged his shoulders looking unbothered.

"What's the occasion for the dress?" Her dad's tone stung like acid.

"Tamar's wedding is Sunday," Sasha explained. "This is my bridesmaid dress."

"Humph. A Sunday wedding? So, I'm guessing you won't be at church," her dad said.

Her shoulders felt heavy from the disappointment in his voice. "No, I won't be there. Ebony's leading the Women in Prosperity ministry until my job slows down. Right now, between me trying to get this promotion, my business trips to Atlanta, and Tamar's wedding, I'm swamped."

Her father scrunched his face but didn't comment.

"We understand, and you're planning your own wedding. This gown looks nice on you," her mother said, touching the fabric. "Fits you perfectly. Ebony did an excellent job, and I'm loving the color. Doesn't it look good on her, Damien?"

With his attention on Sasha, Damien got up and crossed the room, closing the space between them as he examined her in the dress. "Yes, she looks stunning. But she always does."

Sasha forced her pouty lips to smile. "Thank you," she said, taking a moment to observe his well-sculpted physique. Even in his camouflage cargo pants and black t-shirt, he could turn a few heads any day. But she refused to allow his striking appearance or cotton candy sweet talk to woo her. The fact remained; he had disrespected her, and their wedding was off. If he couldn't be faithful to her for 365 days, how in the world could he commit to a lifetime?

He stretched out his arms for an embrace, and her skin bristled. Just the thought of his touch made her cringe. At the same time, she knew if she avoided his hug, it would raise questions from her parents that she didn't feel like discussing. She'd just have to play this one out.

Her back stiff, she allowed him to wrap his arms around her briefly and then stepped back. "I...uh, I didn't know you were coming down today. You usually call first."

"I guess I'll take the hit for that," her father said. "I kinda encouraged him to come since I needed his help with planning the youth activities." Lifting his head, he asked "Is that your famous chicken noodle soup I smell?"

"It sure is," her mother said. "Go on and get a bowl. You, too, Damien. It's good and hot."

The bishop ladled soup in a bowl and said, "I'm thinking about combining the Women in Prosperity group with Damien's Healthy Generation ministry. That way the women can learn to cook healthier meals."

"You're taking away my ministry?" Sasha asked.

"You're out of town all the time, so how can you lead it?"

"Dad, like I've said, I'm working on my schedule. I need a little more time. In the meantime, Ebony is helping out."

"I'll see how things go in a couple of months." He cast a glance at Damien. "This young man has been helping me put together a youth table tennis group at the church and a cooking class. You know that idea's been on my list for some time, and thanks to him, it's finally happening."

The look on her father's face wasn't a good sign. It made her nauseous. Damien had already gained favor by being in the Marines, the same branch her father had served in. Now he was using his professional table tennis skills and cooking finesse to gain more brownie points. There was no telling what he'd told Dad, but it was probably anything but the truth. It sickened her.

Sasha cut her eyes at Damien. "How often will you be at the church?"

"I'm not sure yet. If I can, maybe three weekends a month, unless I have a tennis match."

"Yep," her father said, giving Damien two sturdy pats on his back. "Damien is gonna be a big blessing to our church. With his expertise, we can recruit the right instructors to train the kids. And the older ones can help teach, then it's not all on him. But until he recruits some help, I expect you to be his backbone." The bishop glanced at Sasha and folded his arms.

Her mom creased her forehead. "Is something wrong, dear?"

Sasha tried to soften her distorted expression. "I'm fine."

"You look tired. Are you sure you're okay?" Mom asked.

Sasha was more than tired, she was outright flustered. And the looks her father kept giving her made her uneasy. What exactly did Damien tell him?

Her mother carried a cup of coffee to the dining room table and took a seat. "Help yourselves to coffee. I made a fresh pot."

"Thank you, ma'am," Damien said, making eye contact with Sasha as he set his bowl of soup on the dining room table.

"Guess what?" Her mother said. "I was out on the porch before the rain began, and my neighbor Essie came out smiling. Her son and his wife just had a baby girl. Now that's all she's talking about."

Sasha tousled her hair and blew out a sigh. "Mom, please—"

Her mother cleared her throat, cutting her off. "Damien, I told Sasha you two should go honeymooning for at least a week or two. I also told her that maybe...just maybe, you all may want to do some family planning too."

"Mama, I'm fine with that idea," Damien said with a smug grin. "It's Sasha who needs convincing."

A hot warmth spread across Sasha's face then down her entire body. She wiped her damp forehead. *I've got to get out of here.* "Excuse me," Sasha said, "but I...I need to take this dress off."

Chapter 8

Sasha hurried to the bedroom and closed the door. She was so uncomfortable with this nonsense. Nothing bothered her more than fake feelings, fake anything. And playing the consummate fiancé, talking marriage and babies was all fake. Three to one. Her mom, and especially her dad, loved Damien because he would be the son-in-law that substituted for the son he'd never had, and he'd also become the sperm donor for Mom's future grandbabies. Her mother had harped relentlessly about babies more than usual lately, and she could be worse than a pesky itch when she had a desire for something.

Sasha's anxiety increased as she struggled with the zipper. "Huh! Nobody ever asked me what I wanted." What about her dreams, her goals, her desires? Instead, they had plotted the ideal roadmap for her life, and it bugged her to no end.

She stretched her arms and arched her back again but could not unzip the gown. She tugged and got the zipper to move about an inch, and then it refused to go any further.

"Oh crap, now I have to get Mom in here. Mom!" Her mother didn't respond so she called her name a little louder.

She leaned her head out the door. "Can you come help me out this dress? The zipper's stuck."

She got a response, but with the buzz of conversation and the TV going, she wasn't quite sure what her mother had said. So, she waited patiently in the room, wanting to tug at the zipper but afraid she might break it.

She heard footsteps coming up the hallway and then the door closed. "I was taking it off," she explained, "but the zipper must've gotten caught in the..." She turned to face Damien and felt every muscle in her face stiffen. She sneered at him and pointed to the door. "Get. Out!"

His hands went up in the air as he came closer. "I'm here to help you with the dress."

"I didn't call you. I don't want you anywhere near me."

"Your mother sent me."

"Yeah, well go tell her you couldn't fix it."

He sighed and took a step back, looking down at his feet. "You're being really immature right now. Not returning my calls, completely ignoring me like I don't exist."

"In my mind, you don't exist. I'm moving on, Damien. You told my father, didn't you?"

"I'm not gonna argue with you, Sasha." He ran a hand down the side of his face and stepped forward again. "Stop making a big deal out of this and let me unzip the dress." He put his hand on the zipper, but she twirled and slapped it away.

"Answer me. I thought we agreed not to tell them—"

"*We* didn't agree to nothing. You came up with that half-baked idea about keeping your parents in the dark, and I didn't argue with you. Wanna know why? Because arguing with Sasha never gets you anywhere. It's her way or no way."

"Oh, so now I'm a spoiled brat?"

He shook his head. "I never said that. You're putting words in my mouth."

"Like I need to do that. What'd you tell my father?"

He glanced at her and bit his bottom lip. "I was helping him set up the ping-pong tables and he started talking about how he was looking forward to officiating our wedding. And... Look, I wasn't gonna tell him, but I couldn't take it anymore. We were in church. I couldn't lie in church."

"What's the difference? You've been lying all along anyway," she whisper-shouted at him then grabbed her head with both hands and looked up at the ceiling. "Now, he'll tell Mom, and then—"

"Just calm down. He's not gonna tell her. He said he's not telling her because... you know... her heart issue."

"Were you man enough to tell him you broke his daughter's heart? That you stepped out on me before we could say 'I do'?" She worked her fingers loose from her hair and stepped closer to him. "Since you wanted to tell him, did you really tell him all the details, or did you paint him a pretty distorted picture?"

"No, I didn't tell him everything. But I did tell him about what happened at the gym."

"So, you told him you cheated on me?"

"No, 'cause I didn't cheat on you, baby. I'm Monica's trainer, but I'm *your* man."

She folded her arms. "Get it right. You're not my man

anymore. And I hope you don't think this little Healthy Generation gig you're trying to pull with my father will save our relationship. Because it won't."

"What little gig? Your father asked for my help and I said yes." He sighed and stuck his hands in his pockets. "Helping your father isn't my strategy to get you back. You wanna know what is?"

She cast a steel gaze at Damien and turned away. The path of resentment had grown stronger after each excuse and she was at her breaking point.

"I'm using my honesty and telling you the truth about what happened. I'm also pleading for your forgiveness. Me and Monica...we kid around a lot at the gym." He stepped around her so they would be face-to-face. "And," he continued in a gentle voice, "I'll admit. I might have crossed the line of what's deemed appropriate. But I've learned from that mistake. And I'm praying that you'll soften your heart toward me because I still love you. I'm not letting you go without a fight."

"And the dating sites? The Honeydrop woman?"

"I was on all those dating sites before I met you. I should've canceled my profiles, but I didn't. I'm sorry about that. Honeydrop... we never went any further than online pics. And if you check the dates on those emails, you'll see those pics were sent before you as well." He held up his hands in surrender. "I have no reason to lie. I'm laying everything on the table."

She looked at his handsome brown face, eyes almost as dark as his skin. Luscious lips outlined by a finely trimmed mustache. He was so close she could smell the tantalizing aroma of his familiar cologne. There was a time when being this close to him would make her melt at his feet, but that time had passed. Looking at him now, all she saw was an empty well-wrapped gift. An attractive man nicely decorated on the outside but inside, there was nothing but a stack of promises he couldn't keep and excuses to explain away. Shortcomings. It was pathetic.

She willed herself to remain calm. "Stop fighting for us, Damien. I can't do this anymore. Come get your things out my house. I've already packed and boxed everything for you."

"I won't do it." He shook his head. "I'm not letting you go."

"I'm trying to play nice, but if you don't come get your stuff, I'm sure the Salvation Army will appreciate your things." Saying mean words was hard enough but staring him in the face and saying them was even harder. He wasn't a monster, and she didn't want to think about his kind heart or how he'd made her feel special, like no one else in this world mattered to him but her. But his charisma, everything about him, amounted to one great big, beautiful lie.

Damien backed away from her until he reached the door. He leaned his back against the door and watched her. Unable to pity the sorrow etched on his face, she shifted her gaze to the floor.

"Sweet lady, look at me."

Sasha leaned her head against the bed post and squeezed her eyes shut. She couldn't look at him. He made it so easy to want to believe him, to want to give them another try. But for what? How many years of hell did her mother suffer at the hands of her father before he finally put his cheating days behind him? How many times had her mother forgiven her father for him to turn around and betray her all over again?

"Sweet lady, have I ever..." She heard a break in his voice. "Have I ever given you a reason to doubt me?" She gave no answer. "I didn't sleep with Monica."

Sasha kept her face against the bedpost and inhaled deeply. "But did you want to?"

"Come on, now. That's beside the point."

"Just answer my question."

"I didn't sleep with her."

"I didn't ask that. I asked what you *wanted* to do." Damien said nothing, so she continued. "Why are you not answering me?"

He sucked in a sharp breath. "Okay. I thought about it, but I didn't do it. We spend so much time apart, me always on base, you traveling. I'm a man, and I got caught up in the moment. That's no excuse, but nothing happened."

She uttered a groan at his weak apology, but she needed to know one more thing. "You said you want to be honest with me? Then be honest with me. What if I hadn't gone to the gym? Do you believe your..." It pained her to even say the words, "your relationship with Monica would've become intimate?"

It took him a long time to speak, but when he finally did, he whispered, "Honestly? I don't know."

She was determined not to let him see her cry. She had shed enough tears over him, and he didn't even deserve the two she'd just wiped away with her finger.

"But I'll tell you what I do know. I know I've never loved a woman the way I love you, and this break-up has made me realize that. When I wake up, you're on my mind. When I sleep, I'm dreaming about you. I breathe you. I live to be with you. I'm not training Monica anymore. Think I'm lying? Call and ask her. I've deactivated every dating site—"

"Stop! I don't want to hear this."

"Can't you understand you're my life? Did I make mistakes? Yeah, I did. Everybody does. I tried to stay close to you, attend some of your social events. But you act like you don't want me around your friends, not even to attend your best friend's wedding."

"Do *not* go there! You're hardly here. If you're not on the base, you're playing at some tennis match. When can you go anywhere?" There was no way he could go to Tamar's wedding. She had become adept at denying her mutual attraction to Wesley when she and Tamar chatted. Talk about a catastrophe. Damien and Wesley in the same room would surely be one.

"All, right. Maybe I should've left the military. You know…to help with the wedding, be here for you. But I can't change that. I have eight months left. I allowed Monica to fill a space that belonged to you only, and I'm sorry for that. Forgive me, and let's move forward because you're the only woman for me. From my heart, I love you. All I'm saying is, don't give up on us. Please."

"I can never trust you again."

"Baby, listen. Please. I can rebuild the trust if you'll give me a chance to fix it."

Oh, my God. How many times had she overheard her father say those exact same words to her mother?

"It doesn't matter now. Just let it go. It's a lesson learned for both of us."

She tried to get the zipper to move again, but it was stuck in the fabric. Dropping her hands to her sides, she glanced in the mirror at his image. Hands in his hair as he leaned against the door, he looked like a man in emotional pain. He walked over to her, and she felt his warm, strong hands on the back of her dress. She closed her eyes as he wiggled the zipper until he freed it, gently pulling it down to her lower back.

He didn't step away, and she was too afraid to move. She was distraught, untrusting of her reaction. She didn't know if she'd slap him, kiss him, or both. So, she remained still, listening to her heart pounding, listening to his soft breaths behind her right shoulder.

Silence seemed to last forever then he edged away from her. The door opened and closed with a light audible sound at his departure.

Sasha squeezed the bedpost tightly. Her attempt to block out all of Damien's confessions of love failed; his words whirled around her head faster than a spinning top. She waited a few minutes before stepping out of the dress and putting on her regular clothes. Then she hung the gown on its hanger, laid it across the bed, and walked out the room.

Chapter 9

The minute Sasha's feet hit land, she called and checked on her mother. She was relieved to hear her mom was feeling better. Her blood pressure was still stable, and she had even ventured out of the house. Positive news, but for how long? Her mother's medications were very deceptive. A few weeks, she'd be fine. Then, she'd be hanging on to life by a thread. That's why she needed to speak with Wesley and see if she could convince him to do something to help her mother sooner. She'd call him after she checked into her hotel room.

She'd chosen to stay at the JW Marriott Hotel in Buckhead near her client's office, and he'd agreed to meet her at the restaurant between 6:00 and 6:15 p.m.

Sasha pulled her luggage through the terminal, scrolling through her texts. She hoped traffic wouldn't be too outrageous since it was ten o'clock. She made her way out of Atlanta Hartsfield and stood curbside searching for her Uber driver in a red Nissan Sentra. She spotted the car and waved to the driver. He pulled to the curb and lowered his window.

"Sasha? Marriott Hotel Buckhead?"

She nodded, opening the back door of the vehicle while the driver got out to place her luggage in the trunk.

"It's the JW Marriott Atlanta-Buckhead on Lennox," she said when he returned to the driver's seat, "and I'm in a bit of a hurry."

"I'm Sayeed," the driver said, continuing to make small talk until they reached the hotel. Atlanta traffic would never compare to the vehicle pile-ups on the 405 Freeway and streets of Los Angeles. Still, Sasha was relieved the trip didn't take long.

A bellhop at the hotel opened her door and she exited the vehicle. The Uber driver handed her luggage to the bellhop, and Sasha exhaled. A feeling of relief settled her restless nerves as she trailed behind the bellhop and entered the lobby. She wasn't normally anxious over business meetings, but then she hadn't slept well since San Diego.

"Hi, reservation for Sasha Edmonds." She handed her ID and credit card to the hotel clerk.

The clerk smiled and checked the computer. "Welcome to the JW Marriott, Ms. Edmonds. You have a queen single, checking out Monday morning. Correct?"

"That's correct."

He slid her a key card and pointed to her room number on the card holder. "Thanks for choosing Marriott. I hope you enjoy your stay."

Sasha returned the smile and walked to the elevator with the bellhop following. She needed a nap before she passed out from exhaustion. She opened the door to her hotel room. Sunlight streamed through the window, and a multicolored bedspread brightened the room. The small corner desk would be the best spot to view the city and enjoy a chai tea and a book.

She tipped the bellhop and inhaled a deep cleansing breath. She could hardly keep her eyes open. She eased out of her skirt, then her blouse and finally, her underwear. Dropping pieces of clothing in a trail to the shower. She stepped into the flowing warmth of an invigorating stream of water, and peace filled every pore in her body. After drying off, she rubbed her skin with Carol's Daughter Vanilla Truffle lotion, scenting the room with its fragrance. She pulled on one of the complimentary hotel robes and walked into the bedroom.

Sasha laid out her navy business suit and a powder blue blouse to wear for the meeting. She set her iPad on the desk and sprawled across the bed. Heavy eyelids and a yawn reminded her of how much she yearned for an extended stay in this queen-sized bed instead of attending a meeting. She stretched and turned on her side. Thoughts of Damien lingered in her head. Unable to rest, she jumped up and looked at the clock. 3:23p.m. "Darn, it can't be that late." She rushed to the desk and checked her iPad. 3:23 p.m. *Good thing my contracts are printed and ready to go.*

Sasha didn't think it would take long to close the deal with the prestigious Douglas Internal Medicine Practice Group. She'd pitched Wexel's blood pressure and cholesterol medications to them last year with no luck. At that time, they preferred to research other companies, so she waited nearly a year before contacting Jonah Douglas again. Jonah handled all the business for the group, and they'd met one additional time before he agreed to present Wexel's proposal to the doctors. Bingo. They decided to use Wexel as their vendor and the contract would be signed today. Big time client, big time paychecks from this group of doctors.

She opened her iPad and noticed a message from Jonah. *"Hi Sasha, in response to the confirmation, yes, we're still on for today. I need to change the time to 4:30. Please confirm."* Four-thirty? Ugh, there was nothing worse than a last minute rearranged appointment. However, to close this deal, she didn't mind since he was meeting her here in the hotel. She tapped out a quick confirmation and slipped on her suit. After a light makeup and lipstick application, she pulled her hair up in a bun then stuffed her lipstick, makeup bag, and pepper spray in the side pockets of her briefcase and dialed Wesley's number.

"Ms. Sasha? How nice of you to call," he said, answering on the first ring.

"Hi, Wesley." Sasha smoothed her hair back. "I flew in early to handle some business before the wedding, so I thought I'd see how you were doing."

He laughed. "I knew you would call. But you don't really want to know about me, you're curious about the new medication for your mother. Am I right?"

"That, too. But you did tell me to call when I got back to Atlanta. Or did you forget?"

"I rarely forget, and you follow instructions quite well.

Did your girl happen to tell you that we're paired up for the wedding ceremony?"

"Oh, is that a fact?" Tamar hadn't mentioned anything about that. But truthfully, with all the Damien drama, Sasha hadn't given much thought to who she would be paired up with in the wedding.

"Of course. I'm the best man and you *are* still the maid of honor, right?"

"Yep, it just all kind of slipped my mind. That should be fun." *Not really, not the way his eyes had been all over her body at the conference.* Sasha was flattered that someone like Wesley Dunbar would be interested in her, but she was just trying to stay in Wesley's circle because he had access to something her mom needed.

"How about we get a bite to eat?"

"I...well...I have a business appointment."

"What time will you finish? We can go for a late dinner."

She was not interested in meeting with Wesley today. She scribbled on a pad, trying to determine how to handle this situation. She was tired, and the thought of a wedding rehearsal tomorrow made her feel even more tired. She'd also have to see him at the wedding party he had planned for Tamar and Xavier.

She massaged her temple. "Umm, I'm not sure yet. I should finish up at say...5:30 or possibly 6:00. But, I don't have a rental car, so—"

"You don't need one. I'll order a limo. Just text me thirty to forty minutes ahead of time."

Sasha didn't know how to respond; she needed him and didn't want to offend him.

"Hello?"

"I'm still here, Wesley. You know, I don't want you going out of your way. Why don't we get together tomorrow?"

"Rest assured, a limo is no problem. I have a lot to tell you. Call me when you're ready. Okay?"

She tried to say no, but no didn't come out. "Okay. I'll probably text you." She ended the call. Sasha had done something she promised herself she wouldn't do again. Say yes when she wanted to say no. She glanced at her left ring finger; she missed not wearing her engagement ring. Her bare finger was a painful reminder that she no longer had a fiancé. She was back to single-woman status. Sasha inhaled, refusing to give Damien another ounce of her precious energy. She gathered her belongings and left for the restaurant.

Twenty minutes prior to the meeting, a waiter approached her table and asked her name. After she told him, he handed her a message. *I'm sorry, Ms. Edmonds. I switched our meeting to the Charleston 1 Conference Room. I'll be there soon.*

Sasha furrowed her brow. She scrolled through her cell for another email from Jonah, but there wasn't one. First, he'd changed the time and now their meeting location. *What kind of game is he playing? Hopefully, he doesn't plan to renege on the contract.* Canceled contracts were rare. Known for her tactful strategies and informative presentations, Sasha's goal included only one purpose, signing on new clients. She grabbed her briefcase.

After locating the conference room, Sasha eased the door open and glanced around. The cozy conference room was well-decorated with plenty of chairs and tables, a podium and a huge screen, but no Jonah. She set her briefcase on the table and poured a glass of water from the pitcher. A tall, middle-aged man with gray hair and a pot belly looming over his belt entered. Sasha thought he had entered the wrong room.

"Ms. Edmonds?" He straightened his tie and placed his briefcase on the table.

"Yes, I'm Sasha Edmonds."

"I'm Dr. Jonah Douglas."

Her eyes widened as she shook his hand. She smiled. "It's nice to meet you. Is Jonah running late?""No, my son won't be here."

"I see." She tapped a pen against the table while trying to unravel the web in her mind. What happened to Junior? He was a charmer, easy bait, gobbled up any information she offered right from the tips of her fingers. Now she had to deal with the father.

She retrieved a business card from her card holder and handed it to him. "I'm not sure what Jonah told you, but we've met twice. This meeting is for contract signatures." She removed the folders that contained the contracts and some company pamphlets from her briefcase.

"I've talked with Jonah, and I'm looking forward to hearing your presentation."

A tense grip on her pen followed a blank stare. "Presentation?"

"Yes, I'd like to hear about Wexel's products and services." He poured a glass of water and took a seat. "I assume you're prepared to present?"

"No, I'm not. This meeting was for contract signatures."

"That's what I thought. Did you think I'd sign a contract of that magnitude without information? I won't sign a thing without samples and a presentation. What in Sam's hell is this about? You folks think you can swindle me out of money?"

Sasha wanted to lash out, but she knew stooping to his unprofessional level would tarnish her productive career. And, she wouldn't give him the pleasure.

"Excuse me. Can I say something?"

"Stay in your place." He frowned. "You can speak when I finish speaking."

Sasha looked him in the eye. She had to take the floor, let her voice be heard. "I have something to say."

Ignoring her, he barreled on. "I'm not letting some son of mine who didn't even finish medical school and half takes care of business get swindled again by another pretty face. I know him too well."

Sasha watched the man work himself into a tizzy. She wanted to walk out. How did she get caught up in a family brawl?

Pulling a handkerchief from his shirt pocket, the frustrated doctor removed his glasses. He wiped his face and studied her business card. "Where'd you get your MBA?"

She took a sip of water. "USC. I did my undergrad here in Atlanta at Spelman. Although, at the moment, none of that is important. I don't know why Jonah isn't here, but I pitched our medications in a presentation last month and left samples for your office. Our agreement was to meet for contract signatures after he talked to all the doctors. Here's the pamphlet I gave him during our meeting." She handed him the Wexel Pharmaceutical booklet.

He threw his head back and laughed. "That's Jonah for you. He wants to be the boss, make the decisions. Honestly, his signature on a contract without mine is like no signature at all."

Sasha sighed. What a waste of time. She could've stayed in and finished her nap or accepted Wesley's offer for dinner at an earlier time.

"Dr. Douglas, our meeting is over. But before I go, let me just say, I am a reputable sales rep with twelve years of experience at Wexel, and I've been the top sales rep in our region for the past five years. Your comments were insulting. And I doubt you would've said those things if I were male or a white female."

He looked away. "I...I didn't mean to take my frustrations out on you. It's just...we lost a lot of money—"

"You don't owe me an excuse for your behavior. Good-bye, doctor." She picked up her briefcase and walked out of the conference room.

Chapter 10

At 6:28, a bubbly chauffeur greeted her in a black Lincoln Town Car limousine. Inside the car sat Wesley in a black suit and lavender shirt, wearing a fresh-smelling cologne. Sasha settled onto the black leather seat as Wesley handed her a red rose and a bottle of Perrier.

"Are you hungry?" He placed his arm around her shoulders.

She smiled. "I'm famished."

"Well, here's the deal. I have a lot in store for us. But first, dinner at Anis Café & Bistro. I don't want you saying I didn't feed you." His eyes beamed as he ran a finger along the side of her face.

Sasha bit the inside of her cheek. "Great idea. But, let me say this. I have work tomorrow so I can't stay out too late."

"I know. I'm working tomorrow, too. You'll get back to the hotel at a decent hour for your beauty rest."

They rode through an upscale part of the city. Many of the homes on the pristine streets looked like mansions. Sasha stared out the tinted window, pretending to be interested in the passing scenery. She felt Wesley watching her and it made her somewhat uncomfortable.

She fumbled with the silver chain around her neck, wondering why they had been in a residential neighborhood for so long. Surely there were no restaurants in this secluded area. She slid a hand down the sleeve of her multi-colored jacquard jacket. Glad to be out of the navy suit and buttoned to the collar blouse that made her feel like some child's nanny, she had opted for this jacket with black fitted stretch pants and a blouse of the same color. "How long before we get to the restaurant?"

"Not long. We're stopping at my place for my wallet. No credit card, no dinner."

The driver stopped in front of a large gate. Wesley pushed a remote he had taken from his pocket, and the driver slowly drove through a winding trail that led to a humongous brick home. Stunned by the size of his home, she wanted to inquire why he had so much space for a single man. Did he really leave his wallet or was he trying to impress her by showing off his home? He offered to show her around, but she declined. The restaurant might be closed by the time they finished a tour of that massive house.

Thankfully, the restaurant was not far from Wesley's home. When the limo pulled to the curb, Wesley hopped out barely giving the chauffeur time to put the car in park. He held the door open for Sasha.

"We'll be ready to leave by 9:00 sharp. I'll call if the time changes," Wesley said.

"I'll be here," the chauffeur said with a sneer.

Wesley pulled out a fifty-dollar bill and tipped the driver whose expression immediately changed.

"Welcome!" The hostess greeted before leading them to a secluded table. Wesley pulled the chair out for Sasha.

"Your server will be right with you. In the meantime, can I get you started with a drink?"

"Caymus Cabernet, please. What about you, sweetheart?"

Sasha bit the inside of her cheek. It grated her nerves when he called her sweetheart. "I'll take what he ordered."

"Just bring us the bottle," Wesley said.

The hostess nodded and walked away. Sasha looked around. "I love the vibe here, but why are we so isolated from everyone else in the restaurant?"

Wesley laughed. "My dear, I get first class service here. This is what I requested."

She smirked and opened her menu. She needed a good meal that would eliminate the grumbling in her stomach, and her mom needed that medication. The waitress returned with their wine.

"How did your meeting go?"

Sasha continued to flip through her menu and shook her head. "I wish I could say great."

"What happened? I thought for sure you'd knock it out the box."

"I did, too. Instead, it turned into the craziest meeting I've ever had." She closed her menu. "I'd been dealing with the client's son, who runs the business side of the practice. Or that's what he claimed, anyway. We had a meeting to sign contracts. But who shows up? His angry dad who goes on a freaking rampage about me swindling his practice out of money."

Wesley's forehead crinkled. "You gotta be kidding me."

"I wish I was." Sasha shrugged and picked up her wine glass. She rarely drank wine, but she needed a good night's sleep after today. "That's what happened. He seemed angry, hurt about his son dropping out of medical school. But, I was just there for signed contracts, not logistics."

"He sounds like a nut case. Did you leave?"

"Yes, after I shared a piece of my mind. I was upset. But it was clear the man had a problem, and it wasn't me. I could have set up the presentation, but I said no."

"Can I suggest something?" Wesley straightened his collar.

"Sure. I'm listening."

"Crazy is what crazy does. Next time make a beeline to the nearest exit," he shook his head. "A sale is not worth injuries or your life."

She could kick herself for not canceling when Dr. Douglas changed the location. "I appreciate the advice."

"How long have you worked at Wexel?"

"I celebrated twelve years last month. Doesn't seem that long, though."

"So why aren't you in a higher-level position? Smart woman, top sales rep for all those years, and no promotion? That wouldn't happen in my company. In fact, I'll have a corporate position open soon. Would you be interested?"

"Actually, I'm up for a promotion, and I believe my

chances are good. The other woman is younger and has only two years in sales."

He placed his hand behind his neck and rotated his head. "Two years? Humph. This is getting good. Here's the deal. You shouldn't have to compete with a newbie. If you ever consider leaving, give me a call. By the way, what's the client's name you met with today?"

Sasha looked at Wesley and shook her head. "I can't give out that information. Company business."

"It could be in your best interest. I know a lot of doctors who work in private practice in this area." He leaned back in his chair. "Well, are you giving up the name? I can always find out."

Why not? Maybe he could help in some way. "Let me say this. He has one of the largest Internal Medicine practices in Buckhead."

"Dr. Jonah Douglas?" Wesley laughed.

Sasha placed two fingers against her jaw and looked away.

"Sweetheart, me and Jonah go way back. I'll give him a call tomorrow."

"No, wait. You can't do that. Remember, this is company business."

Wesley reached over the table and put his hand on top of hers. "The contract is yours."

The sincerity on his face seemed genuine and it eased her tension. The man was wealthy and had an abundance of connections in Atlanta and abroad. If he said he'd get the contract, he would likely do what he said, but Sasha's concern was not Wesley's ability to seal the deal. What would he want from her in return?

The waitress brought their meals. Over dinner, they discussed work and all the changes in politics and prescription drugs. From Wesley's report, the clinical trials for Maxitensin should be up and running soon, but he was still waiting for the FDA's decision on the medication. Sasha received the update she wanted, and the meal was delectable. Overall, Wesley was well-behaved. At least until the limo made it back to her hotel. Before the bellhop opened her door, Wesley's large, warm hand slid down to hers. He lifted her left hand and kissed it, focusing on the one finger where her engagement ring should've been.

"So, what's the deal here?" He asked with lifted brows. "Are you still engaged, or did you simply forget to put your ring back on after your shower?"

She narrowed her eyes and gave him a teasing smile. "Let's just say I forgot to put on my ring the same way you forgot to carry your wallet."

"Oh, so it was intentionally forgotten?"

"That's for me to know and for you to wonder about. Thank you for dinner, Mr. Dunbar."

He kissed her cheek. "Have a beautiful night, Ms. Edmonds."

Sasha entered the hotel smiling, even giggling a bit as she went up the elevator.

She wasn't sure if it was the wine or because she'd had a great time. Whatever the case, she hoped it led to a peaceful night's sleep.

Chapter 11

Sasha exited the elevator of the eighth floor at Wexel Pharmaceutical's Atlanta corporate office. Her phone vibrated as she strolled through the hall. She looked at her cell and gasped. "What is she doing?" She didn't know what to say about Tamar. The girl had sent a text notification of a last-minute brunch on the same day as the wedding rehearsal. Now she'd have to leave work early. She was beginning to think Tamar's wedding day blues or cold feet had kicked in. Not that Tamar didn't love Xavier, but something was going on. She didn't seem to be herself lately. Sasha checked her watch. 8:43. She tapped in Tamar's number.

"Hey, girlfriend. I see you got my message," Tamar said.

"That's why I'm calling. What's up with this last-minute brunch?" Sasha put her Bluetooth on. "And when do you, or any of us, have time?"

"I know, I know. It's just... I feel bad."

"Bad about what? You got this, all right? You don't need to add anything else to your list."

Tamar let out a winded breath. "I mean, I love my friends.

You traveled here and so will Lynne, and my other girls changed their schedules around for my wedding. I want to show my appreciation. My poor wedding planner is swamped with last minute details, and I wouldn't dare ask her to do any more. You okay with the time?"

"I guess. Speaking for me and the ladies, we don't expect anything in return. We're your friends. My only problem is rehearsal is at 6:00, now you're squeezing in lunch too. I don't know. Did all the girls confirm?"

"All but Alise, and I doubt she'll make it. Carleen and Elaine are coming. Slow poke Lynne, you know that girl. She's always late, so I'm fine if she gets to Atlanta period."

"She's not here?"

"No. She said she'll be late but should make it to rehearsal."

"Oh, well. I don't see why she didn't book her flight for yesterday or this morning. North Carolina isn't that far away."

"Girl, what flight? Remember I told you she was driving."

"Girl, I forgot, but cross your fingers. Knowing Lynne, she's getting extra dolled up for the fellas." Sasha could see her friend strolling through the sanctuary, long weave trailing down her back, made up like a movie star. She let out a quiet laugh and covered her mouth.

"You got that right. But can you blame her? There's some fine brothers at Xavier's law firm. Only problem is most of them have wives."

"That won't bother Ms. Lynne." They laughed simultaneously. "And who is Alise?"

"One of my bridesmaids. She's Wesley's twin sister; we've known each other since high school. You've heard me talk about Alise. I introduced you to her at that conference. She was working the room."

"Oh, that's right. I noticed her focusing on everybody in the room then she disappeared."

"That's common for Alise. She's a V.P. at Dunbar Pharmaceuticals. Constantly dropping a bug in my ear about selling for Dunbar."

"Say what? You never told me. Let us not forget the strings I pulled to get you on at Wexel."

"I wouldn't drop the ball on you. You know me."

"If they offer you enough money, I bet you would."

"Sasha, what did I just say? Alise is on the hunt all the time for new sales reps. And don't think you're not on her list, but I'm *not* leaving Wexel. When I get pregnant, now that's a different story."

When she gets pregnant? Tamar hadn't made it to the altar yet and she was talking about babies. Sasha's concern was keeping Tamar in her sales position in Atlanta. They'd been collaborating for the past three years, and some of Sasha's tops clients in Los Angeles came from Tamar's hook-ups in Atlanta. She could respect Alise's conquer by any means necessary mindset but trying to snatch Tamar away from Wexel was downright ruthless.

"All, right. I'll take your word as truth," Sasha laughed. But this was no laughing matter. Sales had to stay up, so she'd have to keep a wide eye open for Alise.

"Girl, bye," Tamar said.

"Text me a confirmation, place, and time."

Sasha powered up her laptop and printed out a report for the sales meeting. She wanted to call Dayle about the promotion so bad. Three weeks had been entirely too long to wait for a decision on a job. Per Dayle, they wanted to interview another outside candidate before they decided. But why bring a third person into the equation when she had twelve years of experience, and Amy had two years of whatever she'd been doing? Pharmaceutical sales certainly hadn't been her greatest achievement.

She pulled the report from the printer and stapled it. Her cell phone dinged. She viewed the screen, expecting another text from Damien that she would ignore. Instead, it was Wesley. *Good Morning, sweetheart! I hope your day is going well. I enjoyed your company last night and hope we can get together again soon. See you this evening.* "Sweetheart? Ugh." Sasha placed her phone in her purse. She needed to consider her response. Making a wrong move, be it text or verbally, could mean the destruction of a valuable friendship. One thing she knew for sure, she wasn't ready for another serious relationship this soon. She picked up the report and her tablet and left for her 9:30 meeting with the corporate team.

Her meeting lasted a little over two hours, which was longer than she'd anticipated. All the corporate executives wanted to hash out details regarding foreign drug distributions, and although Sasha had no clients overseas, she probably would in the future. She checked her office messages first then her cell. Tamar had canceled the luncheon and rescheduled the rehearsal for 7:00 p.m. *This woman is losing her mind. It must be anxiety.* Canceling the brunch gave Sasha some extra time to follow-up with a few clients, but first she dialed Wesley. He immediately picked up.

"Sasha?"

"Hello there. I got your text."

"Hold on. Heads will roll if that happens again," she heard Wesley say to someone. "Sorry, sweetheart, I'm in a meeting. Can I call you back in say...five minutes?"

"Of course."

"Listen, I'm sorry about my earlier ranting," he said when he returned the call. "Sometimes certain employees... Uh, I won't go into that. Let's just say, I compensate my employees well and I expect positive results. When that doesn't happen, I see red. Dark red. And that shouldn't happen often."

Sasha wound a strand of hair around her finger. If dark red was like the tone of his voice with the employee, she hoped she never saw that part of him. "I see. Well, if I caught you at a bad time, we can talk later."

"Not at all. What are you doing for lunch?"

"Nothing. My lunch plans have recently been canceled."

"Mmm, canceled lunch plans? In that case, can I pick you up for lunch?"

Sasha stared at the ceiling. "Another outing so soon? I enjoyed last night, but I need to finish a few things before the rehearsal. Did Tamar email you? The rehearsal was changed to 7:00 p.m."

"No, but that's fine. Since rehearsal's not until much later, get your work done and I'll finish my meeting. Then I'll swing by, and we'll have a late lunch or early dinner. You gotta eat to stay alive, right?"

She tilted her head and laughed. "You know what? Being masterful is your forte. You just don't give up, do you?"

"When I want something, Ms. Edmonds, I tend to go after what I want."

A warm tingling sensation erupted through her body. *This is crazy.* Sasha didn't want to feel this way about Wesley or any man. "May I ask what you're going after?"

"You, my dear. And I won't stop. Now what time should I pick you up?"

She toyed with the idea for a few seconds but felt uncertain about back-to-back dates with him. Her motto was a man shouldn't be led to believe a relationship is any more than a friendship, especially in the beginning. She'd have to let him know there would be no romantic preludes.

"I'll be ready by 1:30. The address is—"

"I already have it. Wexel's corporate office. Before you go, tell me this. What are you wearing."

"Why?" She ran her hand through her curly hair and glanced down at her gray slacks.

"I have my reasons. Now what do you have on? I notice you wear pants a lot."

"And I'm wearing pants today. Why the question? Jeez."

He let out a belly laugh. "Don't worry, sweetheart. After I pick you up, you'll understand why I asked. Look for my white car."

"Okay. See you soon."

Sasha didn't know how to react to some of Wesley's comments. She wasn't sure if he was being sarcastic or flirtatious, but it didn't matter one way or the other. Her plan was to stick close until she had what she wanted.

Chapter 12

Shortly before 1:30, Sasha shut down her computer and left the office.

"Are you calling it a day?" The secretary asked, waving at her.

"Yes, I'm off to a meeting. Dr. Gordon's office manager, Shaun, was out to lunch. Could you please try her again? Next Wednesday at 1:30 via Zoom works for me."

"Will do, and I'll email you after I reach her. Have a safe trip back home."

By the time she reached the lobby door, there was a white Town Car parked out front. That couldn't be Wesley. The driver honked, and Wesley opened the back door. He exited wearing a pair of jeans and a tailored jean jacket. *Oh, no, he didn't.*

Shaking her head, Sasha strolled toward the limousine as he walked her way. "Mr. Dunbar." She pursed her lips. "A white limo for a lunch date?"

"Yes, Ms. Edmonds," he said, hugging her. "Why not? I have plans that I think you'll enjoy, and I can't waste energy on driving. My full attention is on you."

There was a lot she wanted to say, but she decided to hold

her peace for now. Was he trying to impress her? If so, this was a bit much. Still, she stepped into the limousine and fastened her seatbelt. Wesley sat next to her and held out his hand.

"What?"

"Can I hold your hand?"

"Wesley..." A feeling of embarrassment made her blush.

"Am I moving too fast?"

"Lightning speed."

"I apologize."

Sasha smiled. The twinkle in his eye was heartwarming. Feeling as though she'd been a little too tart with him, she added, "I'm anxious to see what you've planned."

"You'll see."

The driver exited the freeway and made a right turn. They traveled briefly down a hilly road until he made a right at an upscale nature park. Lush greenery. Manicured walkways. Gently flowing bird fountains and square-shaped hedges dotted the landscape. The driver parked and opened the trunk.

Wesley guided Sasha to the rear of the limo and lifted a large picnic basket. "Carry the blanket. I've got this." He turned to tip the driver and asked, "Can you return in two hours?"

"You and your surprises," Sasha laughed. He was too much. And he was trying too hard to win her affection, which was cute and irritating at the same time.

"That's why I asked what you had on. Going to a picnic in a dress or suit wouldn't be very comfortable."

"I would've made it work." She walked in step with him.

Sasha looked around. The birds were singing. The sky was clear, and they were surrounded by greenery, which meant spring was in full bloom. As they walked the trail, she inhaled the scent of fresh air and plants, thankful for this serene moment which she desperately needed.

Wesley found a quiet area near the pond and spread the blanket out. He opened the basket and removed gold rimmed china plates, two wine glasses, a bottle of wine and sandwiches.

"So, what do you think?"

"China plates at a picnic?"

He placed a sandwich on one of the plates and handed it to Sasha. "I don't like paper plates, but that's just me."

"Okay, this is too much."

"What, the picnic or the China plates?"

"Everything. Everything about this is so over the top."

He glanced at the terry cloth blanket, but not before she caught his wilted expression.

"Don't take this the wrong way." Sasha was being careful about her words. She didn't want to mess up their professional relationship based on his personal feelings for her. "This is not how you woo me. It's like you're trying to impress me with things, and it's... Well, it's so over the top, it's almost comical, and I don't have time for it."

"Wow, you're pretty blunt, huh?"

"No, I don't consider myself blunt, but I do consider myself a realist. And if I'm going to be involved with you, I want to be involved with the real you. Not the phony you that will make me fall for you and then hurt me when your true character is revealed."

"Why all the premature assumptions?"

"I'm being real. I've been cut all the way to my soul. That hurts so bad, and I will not go through the pain...ever again." She whispered the last two words not realizing her eyes had teared up until Wesley passed her a napkin. She balled the napkin in her fist and blotted her eyes, then lifted the China plate and bit into the sandwich.

"I, uh..." He couldn't quite meet her eye. "Well, for one, I've never had a woman talk to me like that before."

She sighed heavily. "I'm sure I've ruined my mother's chance of getting in on those clinical trials."

"No, no, no. Not at all. I wouldn't dare do something like that because you were bold enough to tell me the truth."

She looked closely at him to see how honest he was being, noting the truthfulness in his chocolate brown eyes.

"You're right, Sasha. I usually show a woman my house, treat her to a nice dinner, woo her with a limo and a picnic and bam, she's in my palm every time." He rubbed one palm and studied her face. "But for you, it seems like it's turning you off."

"It is." She held up her sandwich. "Although this sandwich is delicious."

She laughed, and he joined her. It was a laugh they both needed.

"And if I can be honest with you, Ms. Sasha, it seems like someone's hurt you really bad."

She swallowed and looked away. "He did."

"You want to talk about it?"

"No," she shook her head. "I don't."

"Okay."

They sprawled out on the blanket, ate lunch, and enjoyed the ducks waddling along the shore. For well over two hours, they chatted. Mostly about how he and Xavier, Tamar's fiancé, met and grew up together, but he also talked candidly about his ex-girlfriend, a white woman he treated more like a badge to say "I made it" than a life partner, which was why the relationship ended when the woman started pushing the issue of marriage. Sasha loved their conversation, and Wesley seemed more relaxed than before. His mood was more mellow and carefree. A pleasant change from the buttoned-up conversations centered around the pharmaceutical business.

"So why does Tamar call you a snake?" She narrowed her eyes to let him know she was about to scrutinize and dissect every word that came out of his mouth.

Grinning, his large white teeth stood out like sparkling jewels on his mocha face. "She called me a snake?"

"She did, and you better not tell her I told you." She nudged his leg, which was splayed out near hers. "So, answer the question."

"Okay, okay. I have a past," he shrugged his shoulders, "but who of us doesn't?"

"Continue."

"Annnnnd, when Tamar met Xavier, he didn't fully have the 'dog' out of him yet."

"Speak in plain language, please."

"He was still cheating, okay? And I covered for him... a lot. He got caught a few times, and it always came back on me because he'd have me lying for him. But college kids do silly stuff sometimes. We aren't like that anymore. He finally realized he was about to lose a good woman and that scared him straight."

Interesting. Out of all the conversations Tamar and she had, Xavier's unsavory past had never surfaced. This was the first time she had heard about Xavier's infidelity. Tamar painted him to be a gift from God who was one inch away from perfection. At the same time, Wesley's admission made her think about Damien. Was she cutting him off too quickly? Giving up too soon? If Xavier could change, surely Damien could too.

"I've just watched so many thoughts move across your face," Wesley chuckled. "Talk to me. What are you thinking?"

She dusted crumbs from her hands. "That we should be going. Rehearsal will be starting soon."

He looked up at her. "Seriously, what is it? Did I say something wrong?"

"No. I just..." She sighed. "I have a lot on my mind."

"Him?"

She hesitated, then said "Yes, him too."

Wesley shifted his gaze to his wine glass and sipped. "All right, sweetheart." He removed his phone from his shirt pocket and tapped out something on the screen. "Our driver is on the road, but in the meantime..." He lifted a small round box from the picnic basket and turned it on.

Too Good by Drake and Rihanna blasted through the air. "We need to dance."

"Oh, no you didn't play Drake and Rihanna." Sasha laughed as he bobbed his head and started dancing. Wesley extended his hand, and she stood and danced with him.

"I may be wealthy, but I'm not a square."

"I see what you mean, Mr. Dunbar."

Sasha had so much fun dancing around the picnic blanket with him, both trying to do their rendition of different dances. They looked like two nerds, him dancing off-beat to the music, and her trying to teach him the Electric Slide and the Wobble. She drew a blank on some of the steps to the Electric Slide. But at least they were in a secluded area where there wasn't an abundance of onlookers watching them embarrass themselves.

The limo arrived, and Wesley directed the driver to take them to Sasha's hotel. It would've been a beautiful day if Wesley hadn't insisted on holding her hand while seeing her safely inside. And an even more exquisite day if her ex-fiancé hadn't been standing in the lobby waiting for her when they walked in.

Sasha's eyes met Damien's, and her heart nearly stopped. She gasped and tried to let go of Wesley's hand, but he squeezed and tightened his hold.

Damien walked toward them. "So, who's this?"

Sasha yanked her hand out of Wesley's grip. "Hold on! Before you jump to conclusions, this is a friend. He works in the pharmaceutical business."

Wesley frowned. "That's not your business."

"Man, shut up!" Damien shouted. "You walked in here with my woman! I'm about three seconds away from beating you down."

"Hey, who you think you talking to?" Wesley took a step forward.

"Please, no fighting in here," Sasha wedged her body in between them.

"What you doing with him?" Damien shouted. "You accused me of doing exactly what you're doing."

"No, I'm not da–"

Before she could explain, Wesley interrupted. "Oh, you must be the sucker who hurt her! Man, you don't deserve Sasha."

Damien's eyes bulged, and his nose flared.

"Stop this right now," Sasha pleaded, hoping to extinguish his rage. Damien charged toward Wesley. "No, no!" She screamed.

Damien punched Wesley so hard, the man fell on his behind.

Wesley held his left eye and yelled, "Somebody call the cops. I'm pressing charges against this idiot." He got up slowly from the floor then bum-rushed Damien, knocking him down. While Damien was getting up, Wesley hit him again, and they tussled on the floor until security officers arrived and separated them.

A crowd of people gathered as Damien tried to go after Wesley again. Another security guard held him back while Sasha stood to the side, trembling. "Someone please call the paramedics. Please," she cried. Between Wesley's black eye and Damien's bloody lip, she didn't know which of them required more immediate attention. The whole incident was embarrassing and unnecessary. Sasha watched Damien with the security officer, hand gesturing, pointing at Wesley. Her anger escalated. What could he say to justify his unacceptable behavior? She was relieved when he turned and stormed toward the exit.

Chapter 13

Wesley's black eye was swelling by the minute, and the ice pack didn't seem to be helping. He had refused medical treatment and suggested Sasha change clothes so they could leave the hotel. Twenty minutes later, she walked out of the hotel and into the open door of the limo. Nothing was said about the fight as the driver drove them to his house so he could change, and then to the church.

They arrived thirty minutes early for the wedding rehearsal. Sasha wasn't sure where everyone else was, but she hoped they stayed away until she cleaned Wesley's face. She flagged down a security officer in the lobby and asked if the church had an emergency first aid kit with Motrin since Wesley's headache had not subsided.

The security officer said he wasn't sure, but he would check. Sasha thanked him and returned to Wesley who was seated in a folding chair with his legs spread apart, repositioning a fresh ice pack over his left eye.

"I am so sorry," Sasha apologized for the umpteenth time. "I swear, I've never seen Damien act like that before. That was completely out of character for him. And I hate that I got you caught up in my—"

"Sasha, you didn't get me caught up in anything. You didn't ask me out for lunch, I asked you."

"Yeah, but never in a million years did I expect him to show up in Atlanta. And his behavior." She rubbed her hand up and down her arm, trying to understand Damien's rationale for attacking Wesley. "Are you still pressing charges? I mean, it's on camera at the hotel, so you have plenty of evidence."

Wesley waved his hand in front of him as if he was swatting at a fly. "No, I can't file charges. What he did was an act of desperation. If I were madly in love with you and thought I was losing you to another man, I probably would've done the same thing. I can't fault him."

"That doesn't make it right."

"I never said it was right. I just said I can't fault him."

Sasha folded her arms. "I don't know what got into him. He acted like an immature child." She gingerly lifted the bag from his eye. "Oh, no! The wedding is Sunday. There's no way you'll heal in time."

"I can sit the wedding out."

"You're Xavier's best man. You know he's not going for that."

The security officer returned with the first aid kit. "You're in luck. There's two packets of Tylenol and a packet of Motrin in here," he said.

"Oh, thank God." Sasha took the kit from him and removed a small bottle of water from her purse and handed it to Wesley while she tore open the packet. "Say ahh."

"Ahh." Wesley opened his mouth.

She emptied two Motrin into his mouth, and he swallowed them down with the water. She wished he had gone to the hospital to make sure he didn't have any serious injuries. That's a man for you, too much pride to admit he might be hurt.

"Move the pack for a minute."

He moved the ice pack from his eye, and she used a Q-tip to swab antibiotic ointment on the small open cut beneath his left brow then covered it with gauze.

"How do you feel?"

"Better."

"I feel so bad about this."

"Don't. I swear it was all worth it. You're worth it."

She was by his side, standing over him as she doctored his eye. She didn't even realize how close she was until he said those words. Mesmerized, Sasha studied his face and went swimming in his warm eyes. Wesley stared at her lips and kissed her hand, breaking the spell. She looked down at him and smiled. As the air around them thickened, her heart drummed. This was the real Wesley, not the one who relied on limos and fine China, but the one who could wear a bruised face and look up at the woman who had contributed to his injury with adoration. The intensity sent a chill down her spine. His hands moved to her waist, face tilted upward, lips beckoning hers.

She didn't want to fight it, she wanted to let it be what it was. She moved her face closer to his, already wondering what his lips would feel like meshed against hers when Tamar's loud voice snatched them apart. Elaine entered first, casting an evil eye at Sasha as she walked past. *Oh goodness! Elaine is the last person I want to see me this close to Wesley.* Tamar entered, running her mouth as usual, oblivious to Sasha and Wesley sitting in the lobby.

"I don't care if Lynne is here or not! My wedding doesn't hinge on her presence! We'll just figure it out without her. Hurry up, everybody. We're already late, and I only rented the building for an hour," Tamar yelled.

Elaine yelled back, "But the bridal party will be uneven without Lynne."

"I don't care! I do not care! Look at my face. Does it look like I care?" Tamar shouted as she stomped into the church sanctuary with the wedding crew and Xavier following close behind. Sasha and Wesley walked in behind them.

Tamar looked like a jungle woman. Her short hair was all over her head, and her eyes were red and puffy from crying at some point. She took one look at Sasha, then one look at Wesley's face. "What in the bloody hell happened to your face?"

Neither of them got a chance to respond because Tamar swooned and hit the ground with a hard thud.

After they helped Tamar get herself together, rehearsal started. It wasn't as bad as Sasha expected it to be. It was bad, but it could've been worse. Alise, Wesley's twin sister, arrived during the first twenty minutes of rehearsal. Xavier and Tamar had an all-out war because Tamar was dead set on Wesley being out of the wedding while Xavier was equally set on not getting married without his best man, best friend, more like brother, right by his side with or without a black eye. Sasha checked her watch, hoping they would end their feud before they decided not to get married at all.

Elaine and Carleen stepped out for some fresh air, and Sasha went to the bathroom. Alise had apparently found Wesley, and she could hear them down the hallway discussing his black eye and the fight. As Sasha walked to the restroom, she overheard Alise say something about calling the police.

Sasha shook her head; what a mess. First the fight, now Tamar and Xavier had gotten into it full force. Well, Tamar was doing all the screaming while Xavier tried to defend himself.

Elaine entered the bathroom. "Oh, there you are. They're ready to start."

"I'll be there in a minute. I hope we're not here too long."

"If they'd stop fussing, we'll finish quickly. This started early today at the Ritz. Tamar threw a hissy fit over the food for the reception. I'm telling you, no weddings for me anytime soon."

Sasha freshened her makeup. "She's a nervous bride."

Elaine stood in the mirror pretending to fix her braids. She applied a coating of lipstick and returned the tube to her bag. "She's more on the neurotic side if you ask me. Speaking of weddings. I thought you were engaged."

"What do you mean?"

"You and Wesley. I saw you," Elaine said with a crooked smile. "Now you hot to trot for Mr. Dunbar?"

"Don't be ridiculous. Our relationship is strictly business." Sasha knew to be quiet around Elaine. She was a motor-mouth, had been since Spelman. If she admitted anything to Elaine, everybody on earth would know her business.

"Cool," Elaine said, facing Sasha squarely. "Cause I got my eyes on that gem. Have for quite some time."

Stunned, Sasha observed the smug look on Elaine's face. What could she say to Elaine? That she was attracted to the man who had a crush on her? "Are you and Wesley dating?"

"Not yet, but we will be."

"We better get back inside." Sasha walked out of the restroom and into Alise's cold stare. What was wrong with these women? Especially Elaine. How could she be interested in a man and not tell her friends? Except for Tamar, Sasha hadn't met with the girls often after they graduated. They all lived in various states, worked, and Carleen was married. They had made a pact to have dinner or lunch at least twice annually, but Elaine hardly ever attended. Priority number one was always who was dating, thinking about dating, or in a serious relationship because they had vowed to never date or even look at another friend's husband, man, or ex. She didn't remember Elaine mentioning Wesley the last time they'd all met.

At least the arguing had settled down. Forty-five minutes into the one-hour rehearsal, Lynne walked in. She batted her lashes at the men of her desire and stretched her ruby-red lips from ear-to-ear. The row of men swirled around faster than revolving doors as Lynne performed her catwalk down the center aisle of the sanctuary in four-inch stilettos and a tight red dress. Her curves became the spotlight with her long weave, glossy and bouncing. A tight red dress and stilettos for rehearsal? What was she thinking?

Tamar noticed Lynne sashaying in and quickly shifted her attention from Xavier to Lynne. She crossed her arms. "Oh, no, you didn't walk in here at this hour. Rehearsal's almost over. And you," she pointed at Lynne, "are out of the wedding."

Lynne stopped mid-strut. "What? Are you for real? I told you I'd be late. I drove up here as fast as I could."

"Girlfriend, that's your problem. You knew the timeframe. Why didn't you just fly like a sensible person would've done?" Tamar asked.

"Because I couldn't find a cheap flight. But you already know this. We talked about it, Tamar." Lynne pouted.

Elaine stepped in. "She did mention having problems with the flights. We need her, Tamar." She turned to the other bridesmaids. "Do you agree, ladies?"

A frown crossed Carleen's honey brown, freckled face. The quiet, soft spoken one in the group, she pushed her oversized cat-eye glasses up on her nose and glanced at Sasha. "What do you think?"

Before Sasha could answer, Tamar interjected. "It doesn't matter what anyone else thinks. It's my wedding," she jabbed her finger in her chest. "And I say no. If she's late today, she'll be late for the wedding. And I'm not having her ruin my day."

"You're being a little hard on Lynne," Sasha said.

Lynne may have encountered issues with booking a flight, but the way she was dolled up led Sasha to believe this was another one of her games. The girl would do almost anything to catch a man's attention. And this whole scenario of waltzing in late and gaining sympathy may have been planned.

"Sweetie, calm down," Xavier said. "Remember, this is *our* wedding. All this chaos shouldn't be happening right before our wedding day. You're tired. I'm tired. Everybody else is too. Let's move on."

"Please do," Elaine said. "This should be a pre-celebration before the real celebration. You two will be jumping the broom on Sunday. Can we get the show on the road? I'm ready for a rum and coke after this ordeal."

Everybody, except Tamar and Lynne, laughed and muttered their agreement. Lynne slithered onto a pew in the front row and crossed her legs, ensuring the men an eyeful of bare skin.

"I'm sorry for being late. I tried, Tamar. Believe me I tried to get here," She wiped tears from her eyes. Carleen went to sit next to her. She wrapped her pudgy arms around Lynne's shoulder.

Elaine got up and handed her a tissue. "See what you did? Now she's all bummed out because of you," she told Tamar.

Tamar rolled her eyes. "Okay, okay," she said through gritted teeth. "Enough of this sniffling and snorting. You're back in. But if you're not at the church two hours beforehand..."

She huffed and cut her eyes at Wesley. "And what are you gonna do about that face?"

"Sunglasses and an eyepatch should do." Wesley smiled and gave Tamar a thumbs up.

"And a trip to the Urgent Care right after rehearsal," Alise said in a stern voice, her coal black eyes drilling right through Sasha. Sasha returned her gaze with a lifted brow. Alise looked so much like Wesley that she could be his stand in if she were bigger. *Tall, large-boned Amazon women must run in their family. Now if she would stop looking at me like I have three heads, I'll be fine.*

Sasha hadn't heard all the conversation between Wesley and Alise, but she assumed whatever he told her concerned her enough to encourage medical treatment.

After Tamar approved Lynne's participation, a whole forty minutes of rehearsal was added to revise the bridal walk back to its original state.

Talk about chaos. There was only one thing that made it all bearable. As the maid-of-honor and the best man, Sasha and Wesley were paired together, and every time they walked up the aisle, he kneeled on the carpet in front of her and kissed the back of her hand. And whenever he kissed the back of her hand, she felt like he was kissing her lips and butterflies rumbled in her stomach. He knew the effect he was having on her too, because each time he stood to his feet and gave her a scant smile with a twinkle in his eye that said, 'Yeah, I know what I'm doing to you.'

Chapter 14

Sasha spun before the full-length mirror and stared at her hair. Winding a bushel of tight curls around her finger, she turned her head sideways and grimaced. What was taking the hair stylist so long? The woman had rushed out to her car to grab another bag of hair products, but that was fifteen minutes ago. It didn't take that long. Sasha assumed the woman stopped for another cigarette break.

She plopped on the bench and glanced around the large dressing room in the church. Sunday afternoon, and she was feeling guilty about missing church again. Her dad would surely reprimand her if she didn't go soon. And, she needed to check on her mother again before the wedding started.

The more Sasha tried to focus on Tamar and Xavier's wedding, the more her conscience spewed concerns over her own wedding that would never happen. She needed to tell Tamar the truth, but she wanted to wait until after she said, "I do." There was no need to hover her storm cloud over Tamar's beautiful day. At the same time, Sasha was tired of holding it all in. She needed to tell someone her wedding was off because of Damien's sleazy ways. And Lord knows she needed to tell someone the real reason why Wesley had a black eye.

She was still in shock over Damien's actions. The nerve of him to fly all the way from L.A. What in his head made him think she would be happy to see him, with or without Wesley's presence there? And then to act so out of character. Part of her wished Wesley hadn't been the bigger man. It would have served Damien right if Wesley had pressed charges against him.

If he would go to that extent to see her and "prove his love for her", what wouldn't he do? Did the man have no boundaries? No limits?

The hairstylist eased into the room with her clothes doused in cigarette smoke. "Didn't mean to take that long," she said.

Sasha eyed the eccentric-looking woman wearing thick cat-eye makeup and a frizzy bush on her head.

"Puddin' Pie, you okay?" The stylist removed her supplies from a large gray bag.

Intentionally softening her features, Sasha smiled and followed it with a cheerful laugh. "I'm fine...excited. My best friend is getting married today!"

"Yes, honey, yes," the hair stylist giggled. "And you're also getting married soon, I heard. Feel free to hire me for your special day too. I'll fly out to L.A. if the price is right."

Sasha smiled awkwardly. "I'll remember that."

"You okay with an upsweep? I can fix you up real pretty."

"That's fine." Sasha settled down in the chair and held her head high.

It didn't take the woman long to have Sasha primped, polished, and ready to go.

"There. All finished." The hair stylist handed Sasha a large mirror. "Whatcha think?"

Sasha pulled the mirror in front of her face and stared. She held it up for a back view. Her upswept curls were pinned on one side with violet and lavender flowers.

"Miraculous! Thank you; this is awesome."

"No problem. Now let me tighten your makeup and paint those plump Kerry Washington smackers and I'm done." She twisted the wand from the lipstick tube and brushed Tahiti Mauve-Rose across Sasha's lips.

"All righty, Puddin' Pie, you're ready for the red carpet."

After accepting a tip from Sasha, the stylist packed up her supplies and left the room. Almost on cue, Sasha's cell phone rang. She looked at the caller ID, and her heartbeat accelerated. There was no way her boss would be calling on a Sunday unless she was calling to let her know she got the position.

Excited and nervous, Sasha answered the phone. "Hello? Dayle? Hello?"

"Hi Sasha, can you hear me? I'm sorry, my phone was muted. Do you have a minute to talk?"

"Do I have a minute? Of course, I do," she chuckled.

"You know what? Maybe I should wait until you get back," Dayle said. "I just got a bit anxious at the news and thought you should know. You're at a wedding, right?"

"Yeah, but the wedding doesn't start until another hour.

We have time. Shoot, I'm listening." Sasha grinned until her face hurt.

Dayle hesitated. "I'm sorry, Sasha. You didn't get the promotion."

Obviously, she'd heard wrong. "Can you say that again, Dayle? My connection's a little fuzzy."

Sasha heard a light tap on the door and then it opened. Wesley stalled in the doorway looking suave. Sasha gestured him to enter the room. The black, three-piece tuxedo with its silver accents accentuated his large physique. He was wearing designer shades to hide his eye, but she couldn't focus on him now. Dayle's words had just sucker-punched her in the gut.

"...and it made me so upset that I felt you should hear from me first," Dayle rambled on. "A lot of people around here are talking. It's senseless. I'm not sure of the criteria used for the decision."

"I'm sure people are talking. I earned that position and you know it. I can't believe this."

"I know, and I understand your frustration."

Sasha refused to look at Wesley who had sat beside her on the chaise. She clenched the phone in her hand so tightly, her fingers were going numb. "How could they choose someone outside the company?" Sasha's voice tremored.

"Well... actually, Amy McCullen is the new regional director. I don't know what to say. Mike and I feel bad about this. You deserved that job. The sales team was rooting for you."

Saliva thickened to a lump in her throat. Amy McCullen?

She couldn't believe corporate chose Amy McCullen. Amy, who'd been there a hair-strand longer than the junior sales representatives in their department. Amy couldn't string together a decent sales proposal if her life depended on one. And they decided she would be the best candidate over Sasha and another outside candidate who was supposedly also well-qualified? Unbelievable.

"I shouldn't have called..."

"No, you shouldn't have. Nobody wants to hear that kind of news on a day that's supposed to be special. Enjoy the rest of your weekend, Dayle." She ended the call and covered her face with her hands. A whole career of hard work for nothing. She closed her eyes, fighting the hurt and disappointment. Wesley tried to hold her, attempting to console her with his muscular arms. But she kept pushing him away until finally, he lifted her like a child and pulled her onto his lap, holding her against his broad chest.

"You're hurting. It'll be okay," he said, rocking her gently. "It'll all work out."

She knew he was holding her to provide consolation, but his touch was enchanting. And the scent of him, the musk cologne pressed into her nostrils, his large hand rubbing up and down her spine, skin touching skin against her thin slip, set her senses on fire. She reached for her bed jacket and wrapped it around her shoulders. He slid it off and set it on the chaise.

"I've worked so hard. And they bypassed me for... Ugh, I just can't."

"Shh, shh," he said softly. "You've got to believe God has better in store for you."

"Yeah and when one door closes, He opens another," she said sarcastically.

"But that's the truth." He held her hand, the one that no longer wore a ring. "Isn't that what He did with your engagement?"

It took her a minute to realize he was referring to himself as the open door. Discomfort edged in, and she gingerly twisted her hand out of his.

"Wesley..."

"I couldn't stop thinking about you last night, about the kiss we never shared."

She found it harder and harder to breathe while he was talking to her, his voice a low drum, his brown eyes searching her own, face so close to hers.

"You're doing something to me," he told her in a whisper, "that no other woman has ever done."

"Can we just take things slow?" She asked softly. "I'm not ready yet."

"I know. You're upset and can't absorb what I'm saying. We'll talk later about a corporate job for you. And about us."

Even as he said the words, his lips descended upon hers and she couldn't stop him. Didn't want to stop him. She had dreamed of this kiss and wanted it too. His soft lips brushed across hers. She moaned so loud she embarrassed herself, but he didn't give her time to stay embarrassed. Wesley went all the way with the kiss; his lips moved from her bottom lip to her top one, then he held the back of her head and deepened the kiss.

"What are you two doing?"

It was more a shriek than a question, but the words ripped them apart.

Sasha looked up at Tamar's distorted dark brown face. She could feel her own face burning as though someone had set it on fire. She quickly grabbed her robe and put it on.

"Sasha Edmonds, I'm appalled! What are you doing? I told you not to fall for Wesley's charms. You're an engaged woman, and your wedding is months away. Or have you forgotten? Are you even thinking about Damien? Your future? You're throwing everything away."

"Wait just a minute," Sasha said.

"No! Did you listen to me? No, ma'am, you did not. This man here," she pointed at Wesley, "he'll break your heart. I warned you that he would try to slither into your life." She moved her hands like a snake to emphasize her point.

Tamar slanted her head and gazed at Wesley. "And you, why you playing? You know you're not committing to any woman. And what you doing with my best friend sprawled on your lap like she's some wanton slut—"

"You're wrong, Tamar." Wesley interrupted her tirade. "I care about Sasha."

"That's some crap and you know it," Tamar balled her fists onto her hips.

"Okay, Tamar, you need to stop." Sasha rose to her feet. Enough was enough; Tamar was way out of line. She needed to worry about her own husband-to-be.

"She doesn't know?" Wesley asked Sasha.

"No, she doesn't know."

"I don't know what?"

Wesley held his hands up in surrender and slowly eased past Tamar out of the room. "I'll leave this to you two ladies. See you downstairs in a bit. And by the way, Tamar, your hair looks really nice."

Tamar touched her cascade of tendrils. "Bye, Wesley."

He closed the door behind him.

"Wesley's right. Your hair does look really nice."

"Of course, it does. Charmaine's a pro, that's why I hired her. Now don't change the topic. What's going on here?"

Sasha took a deep breath and patted the chair. Tamar sat beside her, and Sasha revealed everything to her friend, including Dayle's phone call.

"Why are you just now telling me this? I thought we were sisters."

"We are sisters!" Sasha wrapped her arms around Tamar so she could feel her love. "I love you so much. I didn't want anything to dampen your special day. I was going to tell you after the wedding, but you effectively ruined my plan." Sasha released her from the tight squeeze and made a sad face. "I hope I haven't messed up your day."

"No, Damien jacked up my day when he knocked Wesley out and messed up his face. And you not getting that promotion is crazy."

"He didn't knock Wesley out. Wesley got in a few hard jabs, too."

"Well, Damien sure got him good. Walking someone

down the aisle wearing sunglasses is asinine." Tamar's lips slanted as her eyes filled with empathy. "And you and Damien... I can't believe y'all broke up. There's no hope of mending the relationship?"

Sasha looked down at her hands, and then back into her best friend's eyes. She shook her head; there were no words to offer. Damien was past tense.

Tamar lowered her voice. "Please don't risk it all to get the hook-up for Mama Edmond's meds. You can find other ways." She placed her hand over Sasha's. "And don't ruin a relationship to achieve all your high-powered career goals either. It won't replace love, girlfriend."

"I hear you. But me and Damien... I can't."

"I mean, I never told you this, but I caught Xavier cheating, too."

"I know," Sasha slipped on her dress.

Tamar widened her eyes. "You know?"

Sasha nodded. "Wesley told me. He even told me that he helped cover for Xavier a few times."

Tamar's mouth fell open. "For real?"

"Yes, Miss 'I Can't Believe You're Keeping Secrets From Me But I've Kept Secrets From You For Years," Sasha said with plenty of neck action. "Zip me up."

Tamar pursed her lips. "Make that, *Mrs.*," she said, zipping Sasha's dress.

"Not yet." Sasha laughed. She slapped hands with Tamar, and she joined in the laughter. Sasha was relieved this little mishap had not ruined the joy of her best friend's wedding day. She wished she had told her earlier so Tamar could have shared her pain.

Tamar bolted upright from the chaise and frowned at Sasha.

"What?" Sasha asked.

"I'm confused."

"About?"

"If you and Damien are not together, why is he seated downstairs for the wedding?"

"He what?" Sasha screamed. Bewildered, she jumped to her feet. "Call security! Damien has gone over the deep end. We've got to get him out of here. He might try to fight Wesley again."

Chapter 15

Standing in the back while the wedding planner gave everyone instructions, Sasha saw a man in a tan suit resembling Damien walk into the sanctuary. Her heart played a drumroll in her chest as she stepped out of line to get a closer glimpse. *How did he get past the security guard?* He'd called her seven times and sent text messages she refused to read. Cowering behind the doors, Sasha scanned the sanctuary, but he was nowhere in sight. *Lord, please don't let that be him.* A whiff of Damien's aftershave, the warm touch of his swarthy hands on her quivering body came to mind.

"Sasha!"

Carleen's gentle voice caused her to shudder. She needed to get it together. She stepped back in place and peered over her shoulder at the wedding planner, who was attending to the train on Tamar's gown.

"You look scared. Take a deep breath," Carleen said.

Sasha squeezed Carleen's hand. "I'll be okay." If she could be sure Damien hadn't entered the church again. Xavier had a security officer escort him out of the church before the wedding party and guests arrived. She glanced at the other bridesmaids. Elaine's eyes were all over Wesley, and Lynne was busy giggling and whispering in her partner's ear. She must have something on her agenda. Sasha adjusted the strap on her gown. Wesley kissed her cheek before they walked out. Carleen and her husband followed, then Elaine, Alise, and Lynne entered with their partners.

Sasha's gaze pointed in the direction of the wedding party, waiting at the altar for the bride to march in on the arm of her father. She kept a light eye on the guests in case Damien came back. Hands trembling at the thought of him being there, she tried her best to spot the man that favored Damien.

Everyone stood as Tamar and her father entered the sanctuary. Dressed in an elegant off-the-shoulder white gown, sister girl's dress fit like she was born in it. Tamar was a plus-size woman with a flat stomach, and how she managed to keep that was another story. Anything she wore complemented her figure.

By the time she reached the altar, Xavier's expression had 'in love' written all over his face. He licked his lips and gazed at her.

The minister, dressed in a lavender robe which matched the color scheme of the lavender and magenta gowns of the bridesmaids, reached for their hands. "God bless you both," he whispered before opening the ceremony with an inspirational prayer.

The couple turned and faced each other. Xavier stared at Tamar and smiled; he cupped her hand in between his and kissed it. "As the Lord brings us together in His divine sanctuary, I know I am a blessed man. The angel of my life will soon be my wife. We will walk together, trusting the Lord's grace and mercy to guide us through our ups and downs and help us remain faithful to our vows for the rest of our lives."

Tamar reached for the card in Reverend Hendrix's crinkled brown hand and read.

"For my sweet love… Love is patient; love is kind. It does not envy, it does not boast." Through chattering teeth, she struggled to go on. "It…it is not proud. It is not rude, it is not self-seeking; it is not easily angered."

Sasha gazed at Wesley's clean-shaven face, the black mole on his right cheek, and those horrible dark sunglasses he had on.

Reverend Hendrix's final prayer ended the ceremony. He closed his Bible and clasped his hands together, admiring Xavier and Tamar. "Now that Xavier and Tamar have given themselves to each other by the promises they have exchanged, I pronounce them–"

The sanctuary door creaked, and Damien barged in wearing a black tuxedo. "Wait!" He shouted. "I have something to say." Gasps and whispers resonated throughout the room. Sasha covered her mouth and looked at Tamar.

"Where's security?" Tamar shouted. "They're supposed to be guarding the door. Please. Somebody find security. I need him out of here!" She waved her hand in the air.

"Damien! What are you doing here?" Sasha asked.

"Calm down. I'm here for one thing. Well, no. Two."

Damien watched Sasha for several seconds before continuing. "Let me start with the groom since he called himself throwing me out of here earlier." He walked midway down the aisle and glanced around. "No harm intended, but all of y'all are duped. Especially the lovely bride, who thinks she's marrying Mr. Perfect. Tamar, you wanna know what happened at the bachelor party?"

Xavier stepped forward and held up his hand. "Listen, brother, you need to hit the road before I put my fist down your throat."

Tamar slanted her head and shot Xavier a nasty stare. "Bachelor party? I thought you said no to that." She dropped her bouquet and folded her arms. "Yes, tell me," she said to Damien.

"Seriously?" Elaine said to Tamar. "This is your wedding day and you don't have time for this. Man, show some respect and skedaddle," she said, pointing to the door.

"Not until I finish" Damien said. "All the men, including the groom had a grand ol' time at his hot striptease, oh excuse me...*bachelor party*. Sasha, your guy was there, too. In fact, I followed him." Damien displayed a smug grin.

Sasha stole a glance at Wesley, who appeared to be holding his breath. She hoped he wouldn't pass out.

"Dude, you're a liar!" Xavier turned to Tamar. "Baby don't believe him. He's just mad at Sasha and wants to ruin our wedding day."

"Why would I do that? I mean, the beautiful women in here have a right to know what their men do behind their backs. And that fella over there to my left. Yeah, you with the beard. He had his own private party at the hotel with the pretty lady standing next to him."

Lynne rolled her eyes to the ceiling and turned her head away.

"Hey, I didn't have a party with nobody. I love my wife," Lynne's partner said.

"You can't prove any of your allegations," Xavier said. "Now leave or I'm calling the police!"

"Don't think that I can't, Mr. Lawyer."

A young man ran inside the sanctuary, huffing and out of breath. "A lady out there said the security guard went to dinner."

Tamar almost collapsed, but Xavier held her up. "What? He's not supposed to leave! I'm not married yet."

Pointing toward Damien, Xavier didn't need to say a word to his friends. They all stepped out of line simultaneously.

Sasha's heart raced. "Stop!"

She stepped out of line, tripped and almost fell as she ran to Damien. "You've taken this too far. This is my best friend's wedding, and you need to leave."

"I will, but only if you'll come with me. Give me a chance to explain."

She froze. At that moment, everything around her was still, all the guests were staring at her. Was his love so strong that he'd come here and try to prove it?

Xavier and his friends started walking toward Damien, but the minister held up his hand. "Please, no violence.

We're in the Lord's house. Sir, could you please leave so I can finish?"

Lifting her gown to prevent stepping on it, Tamar shook her head and started walking toward the exit. "Go on and talk to him. I need some time to clear my head. I...I can't take this."

Xavier said, "Baby, come on. I know you're not listening to that kook."

Baffled, the minister asked, "Are you getting married or not?"

"First, I need answers about that party," Tamar said as she and Xavier disappeared behind closed doors.

Sasha glared at Damien, who seemed unbothered by his frenetic rage. "Leave now, and I'll text you when and where I can talk. You have five minutes to explain."

"It's a deal. Let me see..." He rolled his wrist and checked his watch. I'll give you up to fifteen minutes to text me, or I'll be back.

Chapter 16

After conferring with Sasha, Carleen volunteered to tell the guests the wedding would proceed in two hours. The wedding party disbanded, clearing the building along with the guests. Sasha was thankful because she didn't think she could handle any more wedding drama, even if it wasn't her own. She had reservations about meeting with Damien, but a meeting was better than a fight between him, Xavier, and his friends. She waited until the guests had cleared the church and texted Damien to meet her in the sanctuary.

She walked past several rows before taking a seat and bowing her head in silent prayer. She tried to absorb and rationalize all that had happened this weekend, but she was puzzled.

A hand on her shoulder ended her reverie. Damien sat beside her and covered her hand with his own. She snatched her hand away.

"Sweet Lady, I know you're mad at me." He gazed intently at her and tilted his head. "Please, talk to me. I'm sorry."

Sasha folded her arms. "I don't want your apologies. What I want to know is why? Why'd you come to Atlanta, and what's up with the tuxedo?"

"Honestly, I came to see you, but when you didn't call me back, I went to Augusta for a few days. The tuxedo? Guess I thought I'd be welcome to the wedding."

Sasha cut her eyes at Damien. "Without an invitation? You should've stayed in Augusta with your family, not crash my friend's wedding. How many times have I said we're over. How do I make you understand?"

Damien's mouth was coiled. "I understand all right. It's him. You think he's all that just because he's riding around town in a chauffeured limo. I may not have his money, but I wasn't lying. He's no different from those other supposed-to-be professional men who got sloppy drunk at the party. They were all over those women."

"Like you can talk." She held up a hand. "I don't want to hear any more about that party, Damien. That's none of my business and none of yours either."

"I was out of line, but you got me fired up and I couldn't help myself."

"I got you fired up? You embarrassed me and my friends."

He swiped a hand across his face. "Sasha, I love you. I'm not perfect, neither is Xavier or his buddies. At least I'm not sleeping with other women."

"That's not the point."

"It is, though. We broke up over an incident that didn't happen. I know what you saw at the gym didn't seem right. But I swear me and Monica kid around. I'm her trainer and ain't nothing going on between us."

Her mind kept rehearsing Damien's bold entrance to Tamar's wedding, and it lit another flame on her burner.

This conversation did nothing to make up for his unacceptable behavior.

"Okay. You need some time and that's fine. Think about opening your heart and forgiving me. Call me when you get home." Damien kissed her cheek and walked down the aisle. He paused and whirled around. "Oh...I forgot. Tell Tamar to think twice before she marries that dude." With that, he left the sanctuary.

She didn't know how to deal with him. He wasn't taking their breakup well, and torn between two men, she was emotionally exhausted. Beyond the pain, deep in the crevice of her soul, she still loved Damien, and marriage was one of her goals. The question was to whom? After witnessing the catastrophes he'd created, she wasn't sure about calling him. Her phone vibrated. It was a text from Tamar asking her to come to the dressing room. When she turned to leave, Wesley was standing at the entrance with both hands in his pockets.

"I have something to say."

"Tamar is waiting for me. I think she's ready to—"

"I hope you didn't believe whatever Damien said. I mean, about me. I saw you two chatting it up."

From his demeanor, she assumed he'd heard part, if not all, of their conversation. She flashed a smile and lifted her hand. "Listen, whatever you do is your business. I don't judge people. And, no, we didn't discuss you."

"Why did you discuss anything?" He snapped. "Apparently, his mind is twisted, and I find it hard to believe you didn't know."

Was that smoke trailing from his nose? Why was he riled up? Although she hadn't seen him angry, she'd heard him use words over the phone that would shatter anybody's pride.

"Well, like I told you. I've never seen him act that way. Uh... I'm going to see Tamar." As she started to leave, he gripped her arm firmly then slowly released it. "Listen, I... I just care about your safety."

"I appreciate your concern. We'll talk later." *Dang! Is he gonna act weird too?*

Sasha climbed the stairs, pondering Wesley's change in temperament. The makeup artist exited the dressing room as she entered. Tamar's eyes were red from crying, but her makeup was once again flawless.

"I got your text. Where is everybody?" Sasha asked Tamar.

"I won't even guess. When a sister needs support, those who care stay close." She sighed and bowed her head.

Carleen reached over and patted Tamar's hand. "You'll be okay, hon."

"Alise and Lynne didn't text you?" Sasha asked.

Tamar shook her head. "It's okay. Alise is probably on the phone doing business. And I'd be surprised if Lynne and Reggie didn't sneak off somewhere. I saw his wife run out the church after Damien's announcement."

Carleen frowned and removed her glasses. "Poor woman. Oh, what about Elaine?"

"Who cares? She didn't text me back. Xavier told me

about the party," Tamar wrung her hands. "We talked, and I've decided to marry him anyway."

The weight of her decision hung in the air, and no one uttered a word.

Finally, Carleen said, "I'm not going to ask what he told you. Whatever happened is between you and him. Right now, the only thing that matters is do you still love him and do you still want to marry him?"

Tamar pulled a tissue from the Kleenex box. "I do. But I don't want to make a mistake." She side-eyed Sasha.

Thinking about what Wesley had reported on Xavier's past behavior, Sasha shrugged. "My emotions are all over the place, so I'm not sure what to say." She rubbed her arms as she watched a tear fall from her friend's eyes. "Look, you and Xavier have been together for a long time. Consider what's best for you."

"Oh, my gosh, and I can add to that," Carleen said. "A good marriage is built on working as a team. God first is the key, then respect and communication. Steadfast faith and trust in God has kept my honey and I together for eleven years. When our relationship strained after two miscarriages, we found the strength to stay together through prayer and faith." Carleen touched Tamar's hand. "And remember, forgiveness is important. I don't know what Xavier told you, but you have to decide if he's worthy of your forgiveness."

Alise and Lynne entered the room.

"Are you getting married or not? I can be doing other things if the wedding is canceled." Alise asked.

"Yes, I'm getting married." Tamar threw the tissue in the trash and headed for the stairs. The other ladies followed closely behind.

From the landing, Sasha noticed Elaine caressing Wesley's arm as the two of them bantered back and forth. Alise coughed, drawing her brother's attention toward the women. Wesley stepped back, placing a noticeable distance between him and Elaine.

"Well, here comes the bride," Elaine said, turning toward Tamar with a smile. "It's about time; I was getting ready to come get you."

Sasha cut her eyes at Elaine. *Who does she think she's fooling?*

Tamar looked at Elaine and pursed her lips. "Right, was that before or after you finished with Mr. Loverboy?" She looked over at Sasha and Carleen. "Let's go do this."

Chapter 17

Following a lengthy prayer, the minister placed his bible on the podium. "Xavier and Tamar have given themselves to each other by the promises they have exchanged, and I now pronounce them man and wife. Xavier, you may kiss your bride."

Xavier raised Tamar's veil and embraced her. Seconds ticked into a full minute as they continued kissing throughout the applause. Cheers rang out in a church full of the same guests that had come earlier and returned at the requested time.

"Way to go, Xavier!" A man cheered.

Two hundred and ten relatives, friends, and colleagues applauded as they strolled down the aisle. Sasha and Wesley followed the bride and groom. Sasha's palms felt sweaty, and beads of moisture dotted her forehead. The ceremony was over, and she hadn't spotted Damien anywhere in the sanctuary. Thank God. Maybe he had gone back to Augusta or L.A.

The wedding party shared jokes with the newly married couple before they all piled into a waiting black limo. After a few hugs and congratulations, Amiya escorted Xavier and

Tamar to a white limo, and they whizzed off to the reception at the Ritz Carlton.

# # # #

Sasha admired the rich four-tier white and lavender wedding cake and the opulent décor of the hotel's Grand Ballroom. Table settings adorned with gleaming gold candlesticks, colorful lavenders, magentas, and whites made the setting elegant. Bouquets of flowers in cylindrical vases filled with multicolored stones sat in the middle of each table. Overwhelmed by a tinge of regret, Sasha thought about her wedding plans. As she glanced at the buffet style setup, the aroma of food made her stomach grumble. She laughed under her breath. Xavier had won his choice of a buffet-style reception where guests could mingle and network as opposed to the formal sit-down dinner Tamar preferred.

Wesley placed his hand on Sasha's back. "Are you still with us? You look tired."

"I am tired, but I'll be okay after I eat."

"We should be eating soon," Wesley said, removing his bow tie. "I'm going for champagne. You want some?"

"No, thank you."

She watched Wesley walk to the table where a waiter was serving from the champagne fountain. Her eyes roamed the room for her friends. Lynne was hugged up with one of Xavier's attorney friends. Carleen and her husband were chatting with the bride and groom. And there was Elaine, making her way over to the champagne fountain. Well, look at her.

"She has a lot of nerve," a voice echoed behind her.

Sasha turned around to find Alise. "What do you mean?"

"Elaine's over there with Wes. That doesn't bother you?"

"Wesley and I are friends. Who he talks to is not my business," she lied, wearing a fake smile to cover it up.

Alise snickered and stared at Sasha. "That's not what my brother thinks. In fact, you're all he talks about lately. But I'm not in his business. I hear you're a sales rock star at Wexel."

"I wouldn't say that. But I'm good at what I do."

"It should be worth big bucks. I understand you're one of the top pharm reps."

"I am, but I don't praise myself," Sasha shifted her gaze to Wesley, who was walking their way.

Alise sipped her champagne. "I like your way of thinking. If you ever think about leave—"

"Are you all right, sweetheart?" Wesley slipped his arm around Sasha's waist.

"I am," she nodded. If you didn't count Damien's arrival, Elaine trying to flirt her way into Wesley's life, and his sister's prying, she was all right.

"Have you two become acquainted?" He asked.

"I told Sasha she was your number one topic lately," Alise said.

Wesley ducked his head. When he finally looked at Sasha, his face held a sheepish expression. He pushed his sunglasses up on his nose. "She already knows I adore her."

"That's nice," Alise said with a smug grin. "Excuse me, I

see someone I know." She turned to Sasha before walking away. "We'll talk again."

Sasha smiled, glad Alise excused herself. She had no idea which way the conversation was going, but Wesley didn't seem too comfortable with his sister revealing his feelings, and she wasn't ready for Alise's pitch to join the Dunbar sales team.

"I'm sure my sister asked you about working for us."

Sasha shook her head. "Actually, she didn't."

"Hah. She will be in touch with you. Don't fall for what she tells you." He leaned into her ear. "I have a much better position in mind for you. And by the way, expect a call from Dr. Douglas next week."

Sasha's eyebrows rose.

"Yes, the contract is a done deal," Wesley said.

"Wow. I can't thank you enough." Sasha kissed his cheek. This was the best news she had heard in weeks. Dr. Douglas's contract was one of the largest she had ever secured for Wexel, which meant a double positive. A huge paycheck and the kind of recognition she would use to validate why she deserved the promotion. She couldn't discuss the contract now, but she would express her gratitude to Wesley later. And she couldn't wait to tell Tamar.

The wedding planner instructed all the guests to gather around for the "Jumping the Broom" part of the reception. Wesley and Sasha maneuvered to the front of the crowd.

"On the count of three, jump over together," the wedding planner said.

After she counted, Tamar and Xavier leaped over the broom. The whole room roared with laughter and cheers as the newlyweds embraced and shared a kiss.

The wedding planner tapped the mic. "Okay, everyone. And now for their first dance as husband and wife, our bride and groom."

The speakers blasted *Thinking Out Loud* by Ed Sheeran. Tamar and Xavier's eyes remained locked on one another throughout the dance as if no one else was in the room. At the end of the song, the wedding planner set a chair near the front for Tamar, and all the groomsmen, including Wesley, joined Xavier side-by-side with their arms outstretched. The DJ put on the song, *Treat Her Like a Lady* by the Temptations, and the lip-syncing and dancing began with Xavier singing the lead to Tamar.

Happy for her friend, Sasha smiled. She assumed the routine was Tamar's idea until she saw the surprised look on her friend's face. Sasha was clapping her hands and rocking back and forth in her seat as the guests sang along to the fellas' synchronized dance steps. The guys whirled around, not missing a beat. Sasha laughed. Xavier was so conservative, and whoever taught Mr. Two Left-Feet Wesley the dance steps were beyond amazing. The song ended with the guys bowing to a cheering group. Sasha and the other guests gave them a standing ovation.

"All, right. Great performance from the groom and his groomsmen," the DJ said. "Once again, congratulations to the bride and groom, Tamar and Xavier. Folks, the food is ready, so please line up and be served."

Wesley and Sasha went through the buffet line and returned to their seats.

"You guys did a fantastic job. When did you find time to rehearse?" Sasha asked.

"It wasn't easy," Wesley said, adding pepper to his food. "Xavier hired a good choreographer, and he worked with us for a few weeks." He sipped his drink and caught Sasha's gaze. With a smile, he placed a comforting arm around her shoulder and squeezed. It was as though he sensed her emotional conflict. And, boy, did she have plenty. She'd lost out on the promotion at work. Damien was acting erratically. And though she was happy for her friend who glowed brighter than a sunny day in the company of the man she loved, ambivalence had set in for Sasha. Would that ever happen for her? Would she ever find the happiness her best friend had found? Even after arguing about his bachelor party, Tamar had forgiven Xavier. Wesley bent down and kissed her cheek which made her feel better. But not for long, on the other side of the room stood Elaine. Her eyes fixated on them.

Chapter 18

On Monday morning, Sasha's cell rang at 6:50 a.m. It was the limo driver calling to say he would arrive at the hotel in approximately thirty to thirty-five minutes. Tired, she could use the extra thirty minutes to pause and sit still. Between the wedding chaos, too much doing the Wobble and Electric Slide, plus two glasses of champagne, her legs ached. Add to that the drama of forcing herself to navigate Elaine's cutthroat stares for most of the night. Not easy.

Grateful for the prearranged ride to the airport, the anxiety of waiting for an Uber or shuttle diminished. Thanks to Wesley. Sasha picked up the phone, called the front desk, and asked them to send a bellhop in twenty minutes. She did a last scan of the room and spotted her pepper spray on the dresser. She stuck it in her purse and waited for the bellhop.

Sasha wasn't surprised that the limo driver was the same one who had taken her and Wesley to the picnic area and the wedding rehearsal. He pulled along the curb in front of the hotel, got out, and opened the back door of the limo. Sasha walked to the car.

"Good morning, Ms. Edmonds. Be careful stepping in. I'll load your luggage in the trunk."

"Thank you."

She stepped inside. A white envelope with her name handwritten on the front lay on the seat. The driver slid behind the steering wheel and glanced back at Sasha.

"Mr. Dunbar asked me to make sure you got that."

"Thank you," she said, opening the envelope. She removed a colorful card with a picture of a small tree. Inside the card, another larger tree covered one side. *Good Morning, Sweetheart. This gigantic tree shows how much I've personally changed and grown because of you. I really enjoyed my time with you and hate to see you leave. I may have good news about the medication trials soon. Call me after you get home. Love, Wes.*

Sasha smiled and slipped the card inside her purse. She pondered Wesley's words and the past several days. She wondered whether there were any trials in progress or if Dunbar Pharmaceuticals was ever going to receive the medication, but she shoved those thoughts aside. He'd been kind to her and had no reason to do something that underhanded. All the incidents that occurred this weekend seemed like a dream. Day by day, a new adventure, whether negative or positive, unfolded. At least she accomplished her most crucial goals–participating in the wedding, closing the contract with Dr. Douglas, and starting a new relationship. Maybe. Now she had another goal of tackling the other side of her life.

She arrived at the airport and handed the skycap her

driver's license, watching as his friendly smile changed to a frown.

"Mmm...sorry. I'm rechecking," he tapped the computer keys. "As I suspected. Your flight's been delayed, Ma'am."

"Delayed?" Sasha shifted the strap on her computer bag to the opposite shoulder. "When did this happen?"

"A short while ago. The plane in Detroit left late. You know...poor weather conditions."

"I see. When's the next flight to L.A.?"

"I'm checking," he said, typing. "Leaves at 10:55 a.m., flight number 3788. Arriving in L.A at 10:42 a.m."

"Oh, wow! That's a long wait." She blew out an exaggerated sigh. "Okay, I'll take the later flight." She waited for the skycap to check her luggage and hand her the baggage claim ticket.

Sasha looked at her phone. It was almost seven. She wanted a cup of coffee and a bagel but didn't want to hang around a busy airport for hours or purchase food there. She texted her mother about the flight delay and called Uber for a pickup to a nearby restaurant where she could eat and get some work done in peace.

She walked into the cozy restaurant, and the waitress seated her in a corner booth. Sasha scanned the menu and ordered right away. After the waitress brought her coffee, she scrolled her Facebook page, laughing at one of her friend's posts. Tamar was right about social media. She had made several business contacts and reconnected with old friends.

Looking around the restaurant, Sasha spotted Elaine

sitting alone. *Why is she still in Atlanta?* Elaine had made a point to mention that she was leaving on the first flight out of Atlanta this morning. A tall male took a seat across from her, and Sasha smiled. That was her reason for not leaving.

She scooted over to the side to get a good look at Elaine's date. *I wouldn't be surprised if she'd slipped one of Xavier's friends her business card.* All she could see was Elaine's mouth moving, until the male slightly turned his head. *Wesley?* Elaine was a real estate agent. Maybe this was a business meeting. Sasha decided to give him the benefit of the doubt, until she saw the intimate way Wesley massaged Elaine's hands. Her heart sank. *Well, that flew right out the window. There's no business going on here today.*

Seething, she dabbed her face and stood, ready to break-up the party. *Nonsense,* she thought before she took her first step. She was there to eat, and she wouldn't let their fling bother her. After all, she had no claim on Wesley, and if Elaine wanted him she could have him. Her eyes repeatedly moved to their table, and when he kissed Elaine's hand, Sasha squinted and gritted her teeth. She needed to leave before she did something she'd regret. The waitress placed her food on the table.

"Uh, I'm sorry. Can I get a carry-out and my check, please? I have a flight soon."

"Of course. I'll package this for you." The waitress picked up the plate. "You need anything else?"

Sasha shook her head. "No, thank you."

When the waitress returned with her food, Sasha paid her bill and tipped her. She picked up her bag and scurried from the restaurant. Relieved Wesley and Elaine didn't see her, she stood outside the restaurant and opened her Uber app. She had four minutes before her driver arrived. Sasha released a long-winded sigh. She was glad Wesley's other side had been exposed, but the truth did not alleviate her disappointment. This wasn't the first time...

Wait a minute! *What kind of fool does he think I am? He's telling everybody I'm his woman and he's out with Elaine?*

"No way," she huffed. "Let me go back in this restaurant."

She entered the restaurant and strolled over to Wesley and Elaine's table, approaching them with a big smile on her face. "Well, well. Hello there, Wesley and Elaine. Surprised to find you here."

Wesley jumped and pulled his hands away from Elaine's.

"I'm not here to disturb your little breakfast rendezvous." Sasha pointed at Elaine. "You, my sister, need facts. I hope you didn't go to bed with him."

Elaine glanced around the restaurant and lowered her voice. "Stop talking so loud."

"Oh, you don't want to hear the truth?" Sasha had her hands on her hips. "Well, you will. You better go get some labs drawn, and I mean right away!"

Elaine looked down at the table.

"I'm serious. And, oh...I'm sure by now you've seen his palace. Now what else?" Sasha snapped her finger. "How could I forget the lies and false promises that he won't deliver? Like hiring you for a corporate position at Dunbar." Sasha read Elaine's distorted face and threw her head back. "Hah! I bet he didn't leave that out."

Wesley's nostrils flared. "Now you wait a minute. I'm not a liar and I don't appreciate—"

Sasha stepped closer to the table. "You don't appreciate what?" She picked up his glass and tossed the water in his face. "That I'm exposing your funky behind to somebody I thought was my friend?"

Sneering, he wiped his face. "Are you happy now? You've made us look ridiculous in a public place."

Elaine lifted her napkin off her lap and threw it on the table. "Sasha, let's talk outside."

"Absolutely not. I've said all I have to say. You said you'd go after him. Well, you've got the gem you wanted. And he's not what you think he is. I'm outta here."

"Sasha, wait! I need to explain. She means nothing to me," Wesley yelled.

"What? You jackass. You said you cared for me," Elaine shouted, arousing the attention of other customers in the restaurant.

Sasha stormed in the direction of the exit with Wesley and Elaine following close behind.

"Sasha, wait. Let's talk a minute!" Wesley pleaded.

A few feet from the on-time Uber car that had just pulled up, she pivoted and held up her hand. "Leave me alone! I don't want to hear from you or you." She pointed at Wesley and Elaine.

Sasha tossed her bag in the car and started to climb inside. Wesley grabbed her arm. "Don't do this. I'm in love with you!"

"Stop! Let go of me!" Sasha screamed.

"No. Give me five minutes."

"Would you stop? I have a flight," she tried twisting her arm from his grasp, but he tightened his grip.

The driver, who had lowered the window to hear what the commotion was about, said, "Sir, let go of her arm or I'm calling the cops."

Wesley released her arm. "I'm sorry. Call me."

She quickly jumped in the car and closed the door. "I'll call you. When baboons start crowing. Let's go." Sasha directed the driver.

"Wow! You okay, Miss?" The driver looked at Sasha in the rearview mirror.

"Yes, and thank you. He's testy today." She closed her eyes and rested her head against the back of the seat. Wesley couldn't possibly have thought she'd waste her time listening to his warped excuses. After she recuperated from his manhandling, the thought of Elaine's face when she mentioned lab work made her snicker. Although Sasha had no knowledge of Wesley's sexual history, if Elaine had slept with him, getting tested for a sexually transmitted disease was probably for the best. Payback was tough.

As far as she was concerned, she didn't need a man, Wexel Pharmaceuticals, or a supposed-to-be friend to validate who she was or make her feel complete. It was time to eliminate everyone from her life who'd hurt her or was not a positive influence. That meant they all had to go. Wexel Pharmaceuticals. She'd resign whether she found a job in two weeks or not. In her haste to sever ties with

Wesley, she'd forgotten about her business matters with him. And Damien... He was holding on by a thin thread.

Chapter 19

Los Angeles

After the plane landed, Sasha picked up her bags in baggage claim and boarded a shuttle to the parking lot. She had spoken with her mother yesterday, and her voice sounded different, less like her perky self. Curious about what might be bothering her, Sasha questioned her mom about her health, but her mom said it wasn't that.

She arrived home and changed clothes then called her parents. Her mother picked up the phone.

"Hello."

"Mom, I'm home. How are you?"

"Oh, I'm glad you called. I was waiting to hear from you. Bishop wants to see you."

"What's wrong?"

"You should talk to him. Damien called Sunday evening; he and Bishop met for breakfast this morning."

"Dad didn't tell you anything?"

"No, he called to check on me, and I could tell he was upset. I'm worried. I know something's wrong, so tell me if you know."

"Mom, that's why I asked you." Sasha sat on the edge

of the couch. "Listen, stop worrying, okay. Dad could be upset about anything. Maybe he's dealing with one of the members. Who knows?"

"I don't think so. He shares those issues with me."

"I'll talk to him. What time is he leaving the church today?"

"I'm not sure. He's usually home by four or a little after."

"I have to pick up my clothes from the cleaners then I'll stop by his office."

"Sasha?" There was a short pause.

"Yes?"

"Let me know what happened."

"I will. I'll talk to you later."

"Darn it," Sasha mumbled to herself, pacing the room. If Damien thought he could clean up his mess by going to her father, she didn't want to see him again. Causing all this unnecessary crap. Both Damien and Wesley had pushed her too far, and she was worn out. She grabbed her keys off the coffee table and left.

She drove into the church parking lot and noticed her father's blue Buick Regal parked in his reserved parking spot.

When Sasha walked inside, the silence felt creepy. She was used to the robust Sunday morning service with a packed house, music, and noise. Today, there was nobody in sight. She walked to her dad's office. The door was ajar, but she knocked anyway.

"Yes?"

"Hi, Dad. I didn't want to scare you. Shouldn't you have your door locked?"

He closed his bible and swiveled his chair around to face Sasha. "Not when I'm expecting my daughter. You can close it now. Iris left to run errands."

"Mom called you, huh?"

"She did." His face was flat. "We need to talk."

Sasha took a seat and placed her purse on his desk. "All right, what are we discussing?"

The bishop folded his hands before him, inhaling and exhaling slowly. Sasha knew what this conversation would likely entail.

"Listen to me before you speak. I met Damien for breakfast this morning. This situation between you two can be fixed. I mean, he's a fine young man with an outstanding military career. Most importantly, he's saved and loves you. Are you willing to throw that away?"

"No, I'm not. Tamar asked me that question. You two must be on the same wavelength." Her head angled to the side, Sasha asked, "Did he tell you about the Atlanta trip?"

"We discussed that."

"Hah! I bet you did." Sasha raised a finger. "I doubt he told you everything."

"Yes, he told me about interrupting the wedding."

"He did more than that. His behavior was rude and unacceptable." She sighed. "One of the groomsmen may be facing a divorce because of Damien. And Tamar...well, she almost didn't get married. And Oh! He got into a fight with a business associate of mine. Now what do you think?" She was so tired of her parents praising Damien like he was the King of Earth. In no way was he flawless . Sasha crossed her arms and waited for a response.

"I know all of this."

Burned out from traveling and the disasters that had occurred, Sasha was in disbelief at her father's defense of Damien's behavior. She paused for a moment, forcing herself to refocus.

"You know? And you still think I should take him back?"

Bishop nodded. "I saw the pain on his face. He went after you because he was desperate. You probably don't know he went home to his parents for advice. And he came to me."

"Yes, and he'd already planned to visit them, too. He should've stayed in Augusta. Why show up and ruin my friends' wedding?"

"Kitten. He called you. Texted. Never heard anything. Love can make you do crazy things sometimes."

Sasha pressed her hands to her temples. This was absolutely, freaking crazy! Damien had brainwashed her father into thinking his wrongdoings were because of her.

"I guess it's okay for him to cheat and lie, too, huh?"

"He said that was a misunderstanding."

"I was there. I know what I saw between him and that woman."

The bishop rested his chin against his steepled hands. "What you think you saw. Kitten, you're a smart woman. Why didn't you stay and let him explain?"

"I'd seen enough, Dad. I didn't need to stay."

"Think about this. All your mother talks about is your wedding. I don't have the heart to tell her what happened."

"She shouldn't know. Unless you tell her... Like you did about your other women."

The bishop slammed his hand on the desk; his light brown face flushed. "Now see here! We're not discussing me and your mother. That happened a long time ago."

"Yes, that's sacred ground. We can't discuss your infidelity, but you blew up my business in a hot minute." Sasha flung her hand in the air. "Telling me who I should marry, when I should marry." She folded her arms and paused. "The real problem is you always wanted a son, and Damien is the perfect substitute. And Mom? All she worries about is having grandbabies so she can brag to her neighbors and friends."

"Those accusations are ridiculous." The bishop frowned and held up the bible. "Have you read this lately? Another topic I want to discuss is service in the church. Work is essential, but it shouldn't replace your relationship with God. Ebony does a grand job of sitting in for you, but she's not the leader. Clearly, you will *step down* if you can't adequately run the Women in Prosperity ministry."

"That's not what I want."

"Then you make a decision...or I will."

Sasha's shoulders slumped. Stunned her father's comments and tone, embarrassment scorched her cheeks as she sat in silence. How could he talk to her in that tone? Gloom settled in the room like darkness after a tornado. Sasha and her father had a few disagreements in the past, but never any quarrels at this level. He had been her go to person, her source of encouragement, but not today. She stood and picked up her purse.

"I apologize, Daddy. This is a difficult time for me."

He leaned back in his chair. Creases around his eyes depicted his discomfort. Pastoring the church while caring for her mom couldn't be easy, and now a disagreement about her personal relationship added more pressure to his plate. She sensed his anguish over their brawl and regretted coming here.

He stared at Sasha and sighed. "It's okay, Kitten. Sit down and let it out."

Sasha placed her purse back on the desk and sat. She dropped her head and glanced at the floor. *If he could just feel what I feel.* Her mind twirled in cycles and landed back to where it started. A barrage of promises within a short period of time, two men vying for her heart. She sure couldn't tell her father about Wesley...not everything.

Sasha tousled her hair with one hand. "I didn't get the promotion."

"When did you find out?"

"I got a call from my manager this weekend. Totally unexpected."

"Hmm. What's next?"

"Uh, I don't know yet." She pushed her hands against her face. "What I can say? I'm hurt. I deserved that promotion. Thanks to my business associate, I closed a huge contract in Atlanta for Wexel. Big-time money for them and me. Only issue is...they don't appreciate my hard work, and I may quit.

The bishop smiled. "If that's your choice, do what you feel is best. How are you going to support yourself?"

"Believe me; I'll have a job in no time."

She and her father talked for over an hour. She shared her love for Damien and the uncertainty of whether marriage would be appropriate right now. She told him Wesley was a friend, not her new boyfriend as Damien had insinuated. And she told him about Wesley's position in his family-owned pharmaceutical company, and the proposed clinical trials and medication for her mother. Shock shifted to relief after her father told her Dr. Matthews had reviewed the information she'd sent him about Maxitensin. His decision to consider prescribing the medication for her mom pending FDA approval lifted her spirits.

"Me and Mom want to see you happy. Stay prayed up; put God first."

"Always. I love you and Mom." She stood, walked into her father's embrace, then kissed his cheek. "Expect to see me in church on Sunday."

Before she reached the door, her father said, "Honey, two last requests. Let your mom tell you about Dr. Matthews' decision. And what I said about Damien? Consider it."

With a half-smile, she nodded and exited her father's office.

Lord, please forgive me for saying yes when I'm not sure what I'll do. What else could I have said? A 'no' would precipitate the next world war between her parents. Thoughts of the display of violence between Wesley and Damien stayed on her mind. Being a pawn between two bullheaded men elicited feelings of excitement at times, yet the pendulum swung back and forth. Guilt and fear tore at the seams of her inner spirit over the discomfort of uncertainty. More time was what she needed. More time to build the courage to fan away the lingering smoke and speak the truth about the man she wanted to be with. How could she if she didn't know? And, time was fleeting.

What about Damien's report that Xavier's bachelor party shifted to a strip club scene? Could she trust Wesley? After catching him with Elaine, she wasn't so sure. She could tell the difference between a business meeting and a date. Wesley wasn't any better than Jared, Damien or any of the other two-timing men.

Chapter 20

Sasha lay flat on her back, staring at the ceiling for more than an hour. She hated to go back to work. Tuesdays generally involved office visits, presentations, and playing catchup on projects she had not completed. Today was different. No appointments on her calendar. She would give anything to have another job somewhere other than Wexel Pharmaceuticals.

Lingering thoughts of working under an inexperienced regional director made her sick. Sick of being bypassed for a corporate job she could perform blindfolded. Sick of worrying about the disasters that were yet to come. She was sure people would resign rather than work under Amy McCullen, and there would likely be a drop in sales, which meant more pressure and demands for a higher performance.

No, no one at Wexel would have the pleasure of seeing her face today. She would call Ebony and ask if they could work on the next Women in Prosperity meeting agenda. She could use some girl time, and she owed Damien a call. Maybe she would even call Wesley, who kept flooding her cell with text messages.

Sasha hopped out of bed and did a brisk walk to the shower. Afterward, she applied lotion and opted for her pink silk robe instead of the cute new black and white A-line dress she'd bought in Atlanta. After threading her arms through the sleeves of her robe, she tied it in a bow and walked back to the bedroom, glancing at the wall clock. It was too early to call in. Sasha spotted her iPad, laptop, and the clothes she'd worn home sitting in a corner chair. Too tired to lift a finger yesterday, that's where they stayed. She hung up her clothes and picked up her equipment. After flicking the light switch in her home office, she gasped. On her desk was a large bouquet of red roses scenting the room with their fragrance. Sasha placed the electronics next to her desk and slowly sat in the office chair. She plucked the card from the bouquet and opened it. Her mouth gaped when she saw her engagement ring taped inside and a handwritten note from Damien. He had been in her home. She'd forgotten he hadn't returned the keys to her townhouse. The card read: *Sweet Lady, please don't get mad. I stopped by, hoping to give you the roses and ring in person. I let myself in to drop them off. You'll find the keys in the pencil box on your desk. I love you with all my heart, Damien.*

These men. All the sweet talk coated with sugar-honey lies was getting on her nerves. Now he knew he was wrong. Why would he assume he could deliver her keys, leave roses and the ring, and skip off? He had no business letting himself inside her townhouse. What if she'd been here with someone else? Like a date. She immediately picked up the pencil box and dug in between the pens and pencils for the keys. She stared at the ring and card, then pushed them aside. "I just can't. Not today." She called Ebony, and they agreed to meet at Ebony's house.

Sasha drove to Manchester Boulevard, made a right turn and drove a few blocks to the street where Ebony's apartment was located. Her door was open, and Sasha peered through the screen.

"Ebony, it's Sasha."

"Hey, come on in." Ebony unlocked the screen door. "How'd the wedding go?"

"Fabulous. You should've heard all the compliments on my gown." Sasha removed her jacket and slid onto a dining room chair.

"Yeah, I gotta admit, I put my foot in the gown." Ebony laughed.

"All the other bridesmaids were a little jealous, but I gave out a lot of your business cards."

"Cool. How many are comin' to California?"

"Girl, you never know. Stay optimistic because you've got talent galore, and it will pay off."

"Yeah, well. I'll be glad when my talent starts payin' off. It's been rough on the home front. That old buggy of mine didn't want to crank this mornin'."

"What's wrong with your car?"

"Old age. My mechanic said it's probably the starter. I'll take it in this week."

"And what's little missy up to?"

Ebony had been a single mom since Asia was a baby. Sasha didn't know how she did it all, but she was a prime example of what women can do when they are determined to accomplish their goals.

"For an eight-year-old, Asia has too many things goin' on. Lately, she's into paintin'."

"Aww, she's got those creative traits like her mommy." Sasha opened her purse. "Hey, I bought some souvenirs from Atlanta." She pulled out two boxes and handed them to Ebony. "The blue one is yours and the gold is Asia's."

Ebony's eyes sparkled as she admired the bracelets. "How sweet of you! Now why you go spending your money on us?"

"Oh, that's nothing much. Just a small token of my appreciation for our friendship."

The chime of Sasha's cell broke the conversation. She pulled out her phone. It was her secretary.

"Sasha."

"Hi, Sasha. Dayle asked me to call. Did you check your emails? There's a lunch meeting today at 1:00."

"Today? I didn't see an email earlier."

"I sent it around 9:04 and asked for an RSVP. Amy set up a mandatory meeting."

"Great timing. I left you a message about being off today."

"I got it. Dayle asked me to confirm with everyone who hadn't responded. Are you coming?"

Sasha's mouth twisted. "I understand, but a meeting scheduled a few hours in advance? Who does that? Sorry for venting; this is ridiculous." It was apparent that Amy knew nothing about management, and her insidious methods of running the department had not gained favor with the sales team.

"I know. Should I check you off?"

"Yes, tell Dayle I'll be there." She ended the call and cupped her chin. She didn't mean to take her frustration out on Eva, but this was unacceptable, and Dayle and Mike would hear from her. Setting up unplanned meetings at the last minute signaled a red flag about Amy's management style. She wondered if this would be the norm for routine business meetings.

"Everything okay?"

"They scheduled a last-minute meeting at work."

"Oh, well, before you go, Bishop Edmonds asked me to cut back on the WIP ministry. He mentioned combining that group with Damien's new ministry. He's running a cooking class called Healthy Living ministry or Healthy something."

Sasha rolled her eyes. "Yeah, yeah, sure. I heard about the cooking classes. First, Damien was planning table tennis lessons, now he's starting a ministry. How? He's still in the service."

Ebony shrugged and lifted her hands. "Hey, don't ask me. When did Damien join the church? Or did he?"

"Aha!" Sasha pointed at Ebony. "You've got a point there. He's not a member, and I can't imagine all this happening. Listen, I'll talk to Dad about WIP. Can you continue running it temporarily?"

"Yeah but keep my name out of it. I don't want Bishop mad at me."

"Don't worry; I won't mention you. I have to go." Sasha picked up her keys from the table. "By the way, the wedding is off for now."

Ebony frowned. "Whose weddin'?"

"Mine. I'll have to explain later. I'll call you."

"Girl, you can't be serious. You and Damien broke up?"

"It's a long story. I'll call you this evening."

"You better and don't forget."

The chatter faded to silence. She could almost read Ebony's mind. Their eyes met. The sorrow etched on her face required no words. "I know what you're thinking. I'll be okay," Sasha said.

Chapter 21

Sasha opened her car door and sighed. She needed to decide if she was going home to change clothes before she went into the office. She popped in a Tasha Cobbs-Leonard CD to swing her mood in the right direction. *Why go change?* She had canceled her overdue "get-together" with Ebony regarding the women's ministry for Wexel's business. Even when she was in Atlanta and supposed to be there for Tamar, it was Wexel's business. There seemed to never be enough time to do her own thing. Now, out of nowhere, a last-minute meeting. No, she wouldn't go home. The slacks and blouse she had on would have to suffice. She didn't plan to stay for lunch, just long enough to hear Amy McCullen's presentation. And that would likely be as dense as her sales presentations.

Sasha parked in the employees' parking lot and saw Amy exiting her car from a distance. Her hot pink pant suit with matching heels would hit the jokes list among the conservative baby boomers in Sales. Amy hustled across the lot carrying a briefcase and texting at the same time. Oblivious to her surroundings, Amy's preoccupation with her cell gave Sasha the opportunity to duck her head without being seen. *No parking lot yip-yapping today.* She waited until Amy left the lot and then got out of her car and sorted through her trunk until she found a pair of black heels. Kicking off her loafers, she slipped on the heels and retrieved her computer bag then headed for the building.

"Sasha," someone called out. She turned around and saw Carmen, one of the pharmaceutical reps, running toward her.

"Whew! I thought I'd be late," Carmen said, breathing fast. "I was in Westwood when Eva called. What's the meeting about?"

Sasha shrugged. "Who knows? Maybe a meet and greet."

"Not a meet and greet at the last minute?" Carmen shook her head. "It's gotta be for another reason. I had to reschedule my client's appointment."

"Well, whatever it's about, I hope it's worth our time."

A small group in the lounge sat around drinking coffee while fomenting pessimism. Chitchat about 'time is money,' canceled appointments, and other complaints about Amy riled a few reps, while others shunned the gossip by hiding in their offices. Sasha walked a straight line toward her office, greeting colleagues with a hand wave. Impervious to their criticisms of a last-minute meeting, Sasha agreed with some of the complaints she overheard. Nevertheless, she had no interest in airing grievances with her co-workers. Her plan was to go straight to Dayle and Mike, Dayle's boss.

At 12:50, Sasha picked up her pen and pad and traipsed to the Executive Conference Room. The scent of food swept the hallway, leaving a tantalizing fragrance that signaled the crew was not having box lunches. Surprised they had scheduled a meeting in the Executive Conference Room, she suspected the management team was here for a special occasion or announcement. The large room, known as the ECR, stayed locked and unavailable for use until important meetings were scheduled. The sales teams also met in there when the head honchos wanted to hash out serious sales issues. To her knowledge, in the twelve years of Sasha's employment, they had only conducted five meetings in the room.

Other employees straggled in a few at a time and lined up for lunch. A buffet-style lunch with hot food in silver chafing dishes and servers waiting to assist was impressive. Yes, some important people would most likely show up today. Sasha lined up, received her plate, and took a seat closer to the front where Carmen was sitting.

Nibbling her food, Carmen glanced around the room. "I'm nervous. A fancy lunch and no agenda?" She nudged Sasha's arm and whispered, "Are they getting ready to fire us?"

Sasha shook her head and cut a piece of her salmon. "Fire folks? Not after spending money for this luncheon." Surveying the crowd, Sasha saw the angry effects and vehemence subside as more people entered the Executive Conference Room. While the employees lined up for food, Stephen Wexel, the founder and owner inconspicuously entered through a back door with Amy. They sat at a front table near the podium.

At 1:00 p.m., Mike walked to the podium and adjusted the microphone. Dayle stepped closer to him.

"Welcome, everybody. We're glad you accepted our invitation. Sorry for any inconveniences, but we're excited and wanted to share some great news we received on Monday. Before I continue, I'd like to acknowledge our founder and owner of Wexel Pharmaceuticals, Incorporated, Mr. Stephen Wexel and our new Regional Director, Amy McCullen." Everyone applauded, including Sasha.

She attempted to efface the dirty words in her head as she clapped. They were inappropriate, and she didn't like them. Yet they infiltrated her mind causing discomfort. Being forced to attend this meeting felt awkward.

"Amy will speak next," Mike said. He and Dayle glided to the left when Amy walked to the podium.

Removing paperwork from a folder in front of her, Amy pushed her long blond hair to the side. "Hello, everyone. I have good news, but first, I want to thank you for all your hard work. It's you that keeps our business growing."

Amy went on to explain how they had surpassed their sales quota for the last quarter then discussed a new internship program Wexel would implement. She said the Wexel Pharmaceuticals MBA Internship Program would provide services to graduate students who are completing their last year in a master's in business administration with interest in marketing and sales.

Sasha had not eaten more than a few bites of food and a Waldorf Salad. Her ears stayed wide open. She wondered who had thought of an internship program, and who would have time to develop and manage the project? After Amy finished her speech about the MBA Internship Program, a rousing applause resonated throughout the room.

"Thank you. Now for the juicy part of our agenda," Amy giggled. "Some of you may not be aware, but we are honored to have a contract with Dr. Jonah Douglas's medical practice."

Sasha's eyes fluttered. *Wait. She's not getting ready to do what I think she is.* She picked up her glass and sipped her raspberry ice tea, hoping Amy wouldn't mention her name.

"Dr. Jonah Douglas is a renowned internist with four thriving medical offices in Georgia. Today," her eyes traveled the room and settled on Sasha as she picked up a crystal object. "I'm pleased to present this token of appreciation to Sasha Edmonds for her outstanding contribution to Wexel Pharmaceuticals, Incorporated. This is for all you do for us, and especially for reeling in that 1.5 million-dollar contract with Dr. Douglas's practice."

Another rousing applause and 'hoot, hoots' from fellow colleagues shocked Sasha. Carmen hugged her, and a couple of the reps at her table gave her congratulatory fist bumps. *One and half million-dollar contract? When did that happen?*

Amy summoned Sasha to the stage. "Sasha, come accept your award."

Sasha could not move. Her legs felt like thick lumber boards weighing her down. The last thing she wanted was an award, and she wished she could tell Amy to cut the crap. They all knew she deserved more than an award. She scooted her chair back, pushed herself up from the table, and scurried to the podium. Amy handed Sasha the crystal award with her name engraved on it and hugged her. A photographer snapped pictures, and Sasha tried to leave the stage quickly.

"Oh, we're not done yet," Amy touched her sleeve. "You're gonna love what's next. You were elected by me to head our MBA Internship Program, and your first intern is here. Roxanne Naylor."

"What?" Sasha blurted, feeling perplexed.

Sasha's eyes glowed when Roxanne walked up front with a big grin on her face. She extended her arms to Sasha who was dumbfounded. It took her a few seconds to compose herself, embrace Roxanne and congratulate her. One positive aspect was seeing Roxanne again after their rocky flight from Atlanta to L.A. Years of working toward the corporate position she had longed for seemed useless. The nerve of Amy to assign her another job without asking first. Sasha exited the stage and walked back to her seat.

She watched the expression on Amy's face, a smile that stretched her lips from ear-to ear. That look. Her contentment in handing Sasha a bag of bones while she carried the pot of gold provoked a rise in temperature. *No way!* Sasha marched back to the podium and set the award aside. She adjusted the mic.

"Listen, everyone. I have something to say. I cannot accept this award because I deserve more than a crystal ornament. More than a small raise, a new office, and certainly not a flunky position working under the person who got my promotion." All chatter ceased; everybody's attention fell on Sasha. She blew out a sigh and glanced at Amy, whose mouth hung open like she wanted to say something but couldn't.

"Oh, come on now. No insults intended, but you all know the truth. And Mike. Dayle. Both of you are pitiful managers. Both of you hemmed and hawed about sales records. Every meeting, all we heard was higher sales. And when mine went through the roof, what did I get? A few crummy raises. You didn't even pretend to fight for me when it came to the promotion." Her hands grasped the sides of the podium so hard, they ached. "I hardly ever took vacation time because I was too busy working to make this company richer. I put this job before everything. My family, my love life, my church. So yes, I'm speaking out, because you all should know I am not accepting bones instead of gold. And I will not bow down for anyone. Give the internship program to someone else." Exhaling a cleansing breath rebooted her drained energy level enough to say, "Thank you for listening. I'm out."

Much to Sasha's surprise, her colleagues arose to their feet and applauded. Roxanne's broad grin and thumbs up signaled she understood where Sasha was coming from. Sasha quickly left the stage, spoke with Roxanne for a few minutes. She rushed out of the conference room before anyone could approach her. Mike tried to stop her on the way out, but she waved him off.

She entered her office and closed and locked the door,

thankful no one had seen the water falling from her eyes. She grabbed some Kleenex and pushed a chair over to the large window for a view of Culver City. Fighting back tears didn't work. She succumbed to the pain that parched her heart, covered her face, and let go. She sobbed so hard, tears dribbled onto the front of her blouse, dampening the material. She bounded from her seat and moved closer to the window, watching the bustle of traffic as people entered and exited office buildings. Sasha bowed her head. She needed peace from the chaos that had disrupted her life.

All she could think about were some choice words for Mike and Dayle for not informing her about this meeting or the Douglas account. She scrolled through her phone remembering that she had not called Wesley or Damien. She read the last of her texts, a more recent one from Wesley. *Hey, sweetheart, what's up? Waiting for your call. Congrats on the additional Douglas contracts. Told you I'd work it all out for you. Love, Wes*

Sasha walked back to her desk and pulled Visine out of the desk drawer. She had to clear the red-eye syndrome before anybody saw her. *They cannot get away with this.* She picked up the phone to dial Mike's office, but a knock at the door distracted her.

"Yes?"

She heard someone twisting her door knob. Sasha was glad she had locked the door to give herself a moment of privacy. Otherwise, she'd be swamped. *Probably someone wanting to talk about the job I turned down.* A light knock came next.

"Just a second." Sasha fluffed her hair and applied a new coat of lipstick. No one would see evidence of her pain.

She opened the door, and Amy walked in with her cell in her hand. "I thought I'd be coming to congratulate you, but I guess that won't happen."

Sasha sat behind her desk and crossed her legs. "I guess not. Does that surprise you?"

Amy sat in a chair next to Sasha's desk. "Sort of. I assumed you'd jump at a chance to excel. You've been here a long time. You work hard, and your caring nature makes you well-suited for the job."

"Then you don't know me very well. Sales is what I'm best at. And I should've been asked instead of told about a new position," Sasha's tone had an edge to it. "I'm not trying to be facetious, but anybody who knows me, knows I love what I do. Calling this...this lunch meeting together," she fanned out her fingers, "and announcing a change in my job status that I knew nothing about? That's crazy."

"You're the best candidate. Your sales track record validates that."

"My track record validates more. And you know what I think? This was all a ploy to pacify me because I didn't get the regional director position. It's outrageous." Sasha leaned forward. "Be upfront. How did you really get that position?"

"Sasha, listen. Does it matter how I got the job?"

"It does to me. Maybe I would understand why I was bypassed."

"I won't go into that. You can keep most of your clients if

you choose to. We'll work together with you as my assistant regional director. That position will head the internship program, and you'll be well compensated. How about it?" Amy said with a poker face.

Sasha folded her arms and peered at Amy. "Your assistant?"

Amy clasped her hands. "Yes, I'm a team player. I believe we'd be an awesome team."

Oh, no this woman didn't just insinuate we could be a team. Not in this life. Sasha got up and walked to the door, opening it.

"That's an insult and I'm not interested." She swung her arm. "Please leave. I have work to finish."

Amy opened her mouth to respond, but Sasha cut her off with a raised palm. "Now."

Walking out the door, Amy said, "I'm sorry you feel this way. But I need your help, so please reconsider."

She needs my help. Right. That's because she can't handle her own job. Sasha picked up her cell and dialed Wesley's number. She had to get the facts about the Douglas account before she went to Mike and Dayle. Another important issue she had not been told, and the Douglas account was hers. How could they sign three more of Dr. Douglas's businesses and not consult her?

Chapter 22

Sasha tapped her fingers on the desk. "Pick up, Wesley, pick up." His voicemail blared through the phone. "Darn it!" Before she could end the call, her phone showed an incoming call from Wesley. She answered.

"Sasha?"

"Yes."

"Hang on." She could barely comprehend Wesley's muffled words as he told someone to leave his office.

"I'm back. What's going on? I've called you several times. No return calls."

Aghast at the sour notes in his voice, she paused to regain composure. "Busy schedule."

Listen, I'm at work and I can't talk long. Can you fill me in on the Douglas account?"

"You didn't answer my question."

"I repeat. I've been *busy*."

"Too busy to check in and let me explain why I was with Elaine? I've texted, left voicemail messages and I've gotten nothing from you."

"True. You were on my list to call today, and I called."

"Your list, huh? I put some whopping contracts in your

lap and this is the thanks I get? Your commission will quadruple; you can do better than that."

Sasha tilted her head. "Okay, I know you're upset about the restaurant situation. Believe me, I was upset that day, too." She had called for information, and he was drilling her like he was doing an FBI interrogation. Not today, not tomorrow, or ever would she allow Wesley to get the upper hand.

"Well, you took off without giving me a chance to explain. Plus, you embarrassed me. I think you owe me an apology and a 'thank you.' And FYI, breakfast with Elaine was for potential money in my hands."

"Oh, you want thanks, Mr. Dunbar. Tell me. How should I thank you? Offer my body on a platter? Like I'm sure my friend did. Give you a chunky piece of my commission I'm assuming I'll get. Or does part of that go to you, too? You see, I don't know. And the reason why I don't know is because nobody bothered to tell me, and that's why I called you. But since your attitude is intolerable, forget it. I have another meeting. Bye."

She ended the call without waiting for his reply and swiveled her chair around to face the desk. *This is not over yet.* She picked up her pen and pad and left to find Mike or Dayle, hoping to bypass the looky-loos and reach the secretary without getting stopped.

"Hey, Sasha! Way to go," Nick said, extending his hand. "Any pointers on getting contracts like yours?"

"Hard work and very few vacations. Hey, we'll talk. Okay?"

So much for that. He was a newbie and hadn't been at Wexel long enough to understand company politics.

As Sasha approached the secretary's desk, Eva smiled warmly. "I was getting ready to call you. Mike wants to see you. He and Dayle are in his office."

"I'm headed there now."

Sasha knocked on Mike's office door and entered.

"You looking for me," she asked Mike. Dayle's gaze dropped to the large mug of coffee in her hand. With all the coffee she consumed during the day, Sasha wondered how she stayed calm enough to work.

"Yes. Take a seat, please," Mike said. "I understand Amy met with you a little while ago."

"That's right."

"You mind telling me what happened?" Mike asked.

"I'm sure she told you."

"She did. I want to hear from you though."

"What can I say? I'm totally frustrated over this entire situation."

"What situation?" Mike clasped his hands together.

"The supposed-to-be surprise position." Sasha brushed her hair back with her hand. "I was embarrassed in front of my colleagues. Receiving an award I didn't know about, not to mention the extra contracts with the Douglas account. And bringing Roxanne in on this really sucked."

"Roxanne called HR looking for an internship. She gave your name as a reference, so Amy contacted her," Dayle added.

"I met Roxanne on a flight to Atlanta, told her to call me

after she graduated. And that's not the point. Why wasn't I told about her call?"

Mike waved a hand. "None of that matters. You're usually so cordial and helpful to others. I can't believe you threw Amy out of your office."

"Come on, Mike. I didn't throw her out. I asked her to leave. It's just... I felt somebody should've told me all the facts. Given me an opportunity to accept or refuse the job and award." Sasha crossed her legs, her foot wagged. "I may have overreacted, but I had a right to express my feelings."

"You owe Amy an apology. No one knows this, but she's Mr. Wexel's granddaughter."

Sasha's shoulders slumped. She clutched her pad, hardly able to form the words to speak. "You let me make a fool out of myself. Both of you knew about Amy."

Dayle sighed. "I found out yesterday."

Sasha glanced at Mike with a raised brow.

"I knew," he said. "As did a few other executives, but not until after she got the job. Amy's relationship to Mr. Wexel was confidential." Mike cleared his throat. "Amy likes you. I've noticed her intrigue with you while she watched you present at meetings. I guess you impressed her. She wasn't even angry with you today, a little disappointed." Mike loosened his necktie. "Listen, working with her can't be tragic. Give it a shot."

Sasha shook her head. "I can't do that."

"Amy got the job; now you know why. If you look at the big picture, being her assistant regional director may benefit you," Dayle added.

"Possibly. I like what I do, though."

"Well, Amy wasn't mad," Dayle continued, "but I understand Mr. Wexel was hot and felt your behavior was inappropriate. Could be a problem."

Nagging thoughts, worse than a prick in her eye, came to mind. Dayle and Mike were malleable. Always willing to do whatever corporate asked of them. Maybe Amy or Mr. Wexel had influenced them to urge Sasha to take the new job.

"Is my job at risk?" She asked.

"Let me put it this way. Don't dismiss the position with Amy until you've thought about it. You can keep your Pharm Rep position, plus they plan to offer a salary increase. Negotiate the money part with Amy," Mike said.

"I can't be bought, and I don't like the idea of being forced to take a new job."

"One week. They want a decision by then. By the way, you'll need to sign off on the other Douglas contracts," Dayle said.

"I'll do that, and I'll also let you know my decision in a week," Sasha wrote something on her pad then looked up. "But I don't think I'll change my mind."

"One more important issue, Dr. Douglas requested a presentation for a physicians' banquet in Atlanta. He should've emailed you," Mike said.

"When's the event?"

"Soon. I don't remember the date," Mike shrugged his shoulders.

"I'll get in touch with him." Sasha got up and walked to the door.

"Sasha, we hope you say yes. Keep us posted if you decide sooner than a week," Dayle said.

Sasha nodded and closed the door. By the time she reached her office, a brainstorm had bloomed. She was convinced more than ever that Dayle and Mike were involved in this calamity. The worst part was she didn't have a soul at Wexel to confide in other than Tamar, and she was in the Atlanta office.

Chapter 23

Sasha finished a project she had hidden in her files for more than three weeks. Distractions with the luncheon and meetings had hindered her movement earlier, but now it was a wrap. She was going to stop by and have dinner with her parents. One of her highlights at least twice a week. Mom had called and teased her with the menu for tonight–corned beef and cabbage with hot water cornbread.

She checked email on her cell before she left the office. Damien had emailed her this afternoon. She felt terrible that she hadn't answered, and tapped out a quick response telling him she was back in L.A., and they'd talk when he came down again. Wesley wouldn't get the privilege of an answer to his multiple texts. She put on her sweater and gathered her belongings, closing the door to her office on the way out.

Sasha was elated to make it to the employee parking lot without anyone stopping her. She unlocked her car and called her parents' home.

"Hello," her father answered.

"Hi, Dad. Dinner ready yet?"

"We're just waiting for you. Thought you'd be here by now."

"I'll be there shortly." She checked her watch. "But, it's almost 5:30, so you and Mom go on and start eating."

"We'll try to hold out. You on your way?"

"I am. I'll see you in a bit."

The drive didn't take long, and within twenty minutes, Sasha was parking in front of her parents' house. The bishop walked outside on the porch.

"Kitten, you got here fast," Bishop said.

"Yep, and I'm glad. I'm starving." She kissed her father on the cheek.

"Hey, Mom," Sasha said, placing her purse on the coffee table.

"Wash your hands and let's eat," her mother said.

Sasha smiled and pumped soap in her hand. That was Mom, always making certain no one picked up a piece of silverware or touched a dish before washing up. She even kept hand sanitizer on the kitchen table.

Mom placed all the platters of food on the table, and they held hands while Bishop blessed the food.

"How'd your day go, hon?" Mom asked, serving herself some cabbage and passing the bowl to her dad.

"Not as well as I'd hoped. My bosses asked me to take a new position."

"What kind of position?" Bishop asked.

"Well, it's a management position. Working underneath the woman who got the position I applied for."

"Hmmm. How'd that make you feel?" Bishop asked.

Sasha's lips puckered. "Disappointed. Upset. They held a surprise luncheon for the staff, and Amy told all the employees I would be her assistant regional director, and that I'd also head a new internship program they're starting. But it gets even better. I knew nothing about the job."

"Excuse me," Mom said. "How could she pull that stunt?"

The bishop wiped his mouth and finished chewing. "Don't jump the gun. Accepting the job might not be a bad idea. You got a raise coming?"

"Yes, Daddy, but money's not my concern. It's the principle. Amy is the owner's granddaughter."

"Heck," Mom waved her fork. "That's worse. You'd wind up being a plantation slave for that woman."

"A slave? That's ridiculous." Bishop said.

"I don't agree. The woman got the job Sasha earned. Now she wants to be her boss?

Ba-a-by, I would've told her where to go," Mom told Sasha.

"Odette, be careful about giving that girl wrong advice. Remember, she's got to keep a roof over her head. The woman's going to be her boss anyway."

"Wrong advice? Listen, Mr. Edmonds, I don't think it's wrong. She'll have to work directly under her. That's different. Right, Sasha?"

"All right, you two. Cut it out. I didn't ask for resolutions. I'll decide what I want to do. Kinda thought you'd both listen for a change." Sasha's eyes shifted to her plate. Whenever her mom called her father Mr. Edmonds, the quarrel wasn't over until she had the last word.

She looked up; her parents were staring at one another with question marks on their faces. They shifted their eyes to her. The proud Bishop and First Lady, accustomed to giving rather than receiving advice, seemed astonished. Sasha placed a hand over her parents' hands. She didn't want them to worry, particularly her mother.

"I love you guys, and I appreciate your input. Honestly, I do. Believe me; I'll do what I feel is best for me."

Her father squeezed her hand. "Kitten, we didn't mean to intrude. We don't want you to lose your job. Just take your problems to the Lord and ask for His guidance."

"Bishop's right, Honey. We'll see you in church Sunday, won't we?" Her mom asked.

"I'll be there."

Sasha shared how she'd met Roxanne on the plane and how they'd comforted one another during the storm. She told them she'd given her a business card for future contact. Her internship threw a wrench in her initial plan to submit her resignation from Wexel. Now everything depended on whether they'd let her stay if she refused the job. Sasha was hoping she could still be a mentor to Roxanne without taking the position.

"Kitten, I can imagine how you feel. That wasn't the best way to promote an employee."

"Dad, I don't even know if it's a promotion. I haven't interviewed, seen a job description or know what kind of compensation I'd receive."

"Doesn't sound right," her mother said, passing the plate of corned beef to Sasha.

"No, thank you. I'm getting full."

"What? You didn't eat very much," her mom observed.

Sasha sipped her iced tea. "It's hard to eat. I keep thinking...What about Roxanne? She came to Wexel because I offered to help her." No way would Sasha allow that young woman to build ties with Wexel and she not be involved. Somehow, she'd make sure Roxanne received the training she promised her.

"Honey, you'll figure it out. Have you talked to Damien?" Mom flashed her winning smile like she'd won the lottery every time she mentioned his name. It was apparent she was still unaware Sasha and Damien were not together. The call to him this evening slipped her mind. Occupied with thoughts of what had transpired today, getting through the remainder of the day was a miracle.

Chapter 24

Although Sasha was tired, she didn't want to refuse her parents the enjoyment of spending time with them. She watched a few television shows with her parents and then drove home.

She undressed and got ready for bed but couldn't get Damien out of her head. She sat on the bed, gazing at her phone on the nightstand. *Call him tonight or tomorrow?* She had agreed to call when she returned home and owed him that much. Problem was she didn't have answers for his questions and didn't feel like getting into relationship issues tonight. *If not tonight, when?* She picked up her cell and dialed Damien's number. He answered after the first ring.

"Hey."

"Hey," she said, surprised he answered so quickly. "Did I wake you?"

"No, I'm up. How're you doing?"

"Fair. Thank you for the lovely flowers and the card. That was touching."

"You deserve them, sweet lady. Did you see your ring?"

She closed her eyes and lifted her head. "I did. I, uh...don't have an answer for you."

"Are you considering? Or is it a no go?"

The question made her anxious. She got up and walked to the kitchen.

"I don't know, Damien." She retrieved a bottle of water from the refrigerator before walking back to her room. "You know, I can't say let's get back together. We should take our time. I have a lot going on."

"Take our time?" He let out a soft laugh. "Baby, time is short. Life is short. I know I wanna be with you, and either you feel the same or you don't. Simple as that."

Sasha had rewound the video and played it over and over in her mind. Visualizing the scene at the church, the fight with Wesley, the other woman. Days had passed, and her protracted anger gradually subsided. She had so many reasons to let him go, but something in her heart kept resisting the idea.

"Sasha, say something. Do you still love me?"

She pushed her fingers against her forehead. "Damien, I'm exhausted. Please don't do this."

"I have to know."

"Why now? I'm trying to figure things out." She flipped on blue tooth, placed the phone in her pajama pocket, and walked to the living room.

"Figure out what? I was wrong, and I've apologized. I went ballistic because I wanted you back. I flew to Atlanta to find you."

"Yes, and find me you did. You screwed up my best friend's wedding."

"I told you before, I was desperate."

"So, now it's my fault?"

"Sweet lady, stop! Why are you putting me through this? All I wanna know is do you love me?"

"Yes," she shouted in the phone. Sasha regretted giving him the answer he wanted so rapidly. "Are you happy now?"

"I'm thrilled. Now say you'll marry me."

"You won't hear it tonight You hurt me, and I'm healing. But I'm still undecided about our relationship."

"Sasha."

"I have to be up early for this freaking job. Let me know when you're in L.A."

Damien didn't respond.

"Are you here?"

"I'm here, Sasha. I'll talk to you another time."

Sasha could hear the disappointment in his voice. Although the call ended in a strange way, she was satisfied with ending the conversation the way she did. No false hopes or promises. Her broken heart would never serve as his bullseye a second time around. She had to be sure before making any moves. She connected her cell to the charger and turned off her bedside lamp. Laying on her back, she closed her eyes and prayed for guidance.

####

Up two hours earlier than usual, Sasha stretched before rising and going into her home office. The call to Damien had sidetracked her plan to email Dr. Douglas for clarification about the date and details of his event. She flipped on her desktop and combed through her emails.

"Oh, wow!" Somehow, Sasha had missed the email from

Jonah last week. The annual Internal Medicine Physician's Banquet was this Friday evening. *That explains why he contacted Mike.* She folded her arms trying to fight the disappointment welling up inside. This meant another trip to Atlanta, which she had not planned to do for at least a month. She would need to prepare for the presentation and arrange a flight out for Thursday. It was imperative she return to L.A. early Saturday morning. Sasha absolutely could not miss church Sunday. She also wanted to avoid seeing Wesley. That was a definite no.

She confirmed her attendance via email to Dr. Douglas, and called to leave a message on the secretary's extension.

"Good Morning, Eva. This is Sasha. I need a favor. Please book me a roundtrip flight to Atlanta for this Thursday, early morning. Returning Saturday on the earliest flight out. Oh, and please don't book me at the JW Marriott in Buckhead. This is a special request, so Dr. Jonah Douglas will foot the bill for my travel expenses. Call me about the hotel if you have questions. Thanks."

Chapter 25

Los Angeles - Thursday

Sasha swerved into the American Airlines parking garage and slipped her credit card in the slot to retrieve a ticket.

She parked and checked her watch. Forty-five minutes to get through security and to the gate. She was thankful she had printed her boarding pass the night before. Boarding Pass. Is it in my purse? She rummaged through her purse. Wallet. Driver's license. Passport. But no boarding pass. She got out the car and opened her computer bag, searching through her folders. The boarding pass was tucked in between some paperwork she had printed last night. She let out a deep sigh and locked her car, walking quickly toward the terminal.

She handed the skycap her luggage at curbside and set off on what seemed like the longest fast-paced walk ever. She knew her mom was up and dialed her parents' home.

"Hello."

"Mom, it's me. I'm at the airport. How'd your doctor's visit go yesterday?"

"Sorry, hon. I forgot to call you back. Your aunt kept me on the phone gossiping. My blood pressure's much better."

"That's great. I just wanted to check on you before my flight. I'll call you when I get to Atlanta. Love you."

"I love you, too, dear. Be careful down there."

"I will."

Sasha was glad her mother sounded much better. She felt more at peace about her mother's health after seeing her recent improvements. Lifestyle changes of modifying her diet by eating healthier and adding more exercise had played an enormous role. And, knowing Dr. Matthews would consider Maxitensin if the current regimen did not continue to help was a godsend. She didn't want any negativity to disrupt her mother's physical or mental wellness.

"Flight 2432 at Gate 34 is now boarding for Atlanta," blasted over the intercom. Sasha's fast walk changed to a run as she navigated around people with boatloads of luggage and a group of laughing teens blocking the pathway. She made it to Gate 34 behind the last two passengers showing their boarding passes, then pulled her pass out from her wallet. Just in time.

Chapter 26

Sasha exited the plane with her Bluetooth in her ear. She had texted Tamar to leave for the airport but didn't get a response. She dialed Tamar's number before she merged with the bustling crowd rushing to baggage claim. Where is she? Next, to Lynne, Tamar was second on her list of "Do Not Call for Urgent Rides." She knew her friend well. If she was chatting with someone, that might delay her trip to the airport by an hour or more. Sasha set her bag on a chair and tied the belt on her jacket. A few minutes later, a text came in from Tamar. Leaving now.

Close to an hour after her text, Tamar pulled curbside and unlocked the door.

Sasha opened the door and gave her a "you know you're wrong" look. "Girl, I said to myself, is she coming?"

"Oh? Since when have I left you at the airport?"

Sasha loaded her bags in the back and climbed in the front. She laughed at Tamar's wide-eyed glare while fastening her seat belt.

"I was joking, hon. But you are slow getting to the airport. Like you don't remember doing this before."

"Yeah, yeah. Beggars can't be choosy."

"Gotcha. How was your honeymoon?"

"Too short. But we'll take another one whenever Xavier can slow his roll at work."

"Hmmm, maybe in two or three years?" They both laughed.

"It better not be that long," Tamar said.

Sasha hoped her friend had insisted on Xavier's commitment to her. He had worked hard to establish a stellar career, and his job as an attorney kept him busy.

"Wait a minute. Where'd you say you're staying?"

"The Westin-Atlanta Perimeter North." Sasha pulled out her reservation. "It's on Concourse."

"Oh, I know where it is. I just remembered you mentioned not going to the Marriott."

"Not this time." Sasha sighed, examining her fresh manicure. "I'm hoping I won't run into Wesley."

Tamar stopped at a red light. Sasha could feel her friend's eyes crawling over her, and that was worse than an irritable itch.

"What?" Sasha frowned.

"What's up with you and Wes? For a minute, y'all were all lovey-dovey. Couldn't keep your hands off one another. Now you want to avoid him?"

"Uh, I told you before. You were wrong about Wesley and me. And what you saw in the dressing room for five seconds was not what you thought. Why are even we having this conversation? I'm telling you, that whole ordeal with him was nothing."

"You two all hugged up was nothing?"

"Nope! And we've talked about this. I was hurt and angry after talking to Dayle. He was consoling me."

"Girlfriend, let me say something, and I'm not getting in your business. I don't care what you say. That man is into you. From what Alise is saying, he's talking about his new woman in public and in Dunbar meetings. Telling folks you're his woman."

"Whoa. I'm not his woman. I didn't have any intention of getting involved with him. And yes, at first I kinda thought–"

"Thought what?" Tamar interrupted. "Thought you'd go out on a few dates and get Mama Edmond's medication?"

Sasha shot her friend a side-eye. "Of course not. I knew better." Well, she should've known better. She started thinking how everything had gone off course with Wesley. If she had used her head, she would have waited until he produced the medication before she let him take her out. A simple date may have transitioned to an attraction in overkill, and she didn't know how to handle him.

Tamar turned down the next street and parked. She faced Sasha but remained silent.

Sasha crossed her arms. "All right, like I told you. We went out to dinner a couple of times and on a picnic. And, for the record, there was a mutual attraction, but I didn't sleep with him." She stared out the window. "Something about him changed. He...well, he started getting possessive, demanding to know when I'd return to Atlanta. I had to stop taking his calls."

"Well, don't think it's over."

"It is. I don't want to see him again. I mean...I'm still dealing with Damien, and that's enough. Besides, I think he's seeing Elaine. I saw them at a restaurant." Sasha chuckled under her breath, although it wasn't the least bit funny. Every time she thought of Wesley and Elaine, she felt like an idiot. A wealthy businessman who was serious about a relationship with one woman? Doubtful. And as for Elaine? Their friendship was over. No, she wasn't Wesley's woman, and she should have disclosed their mutual attraction to Elaine, but it is what it is. She couldn't change the past.

"Please. Wes don't want Elaine," Tamar glanced at Sasha. "Tell that man how you feel and end the relationship on a good note."

"A good note?" Sasha's brows furrowed. "After what I saw, I don't need to tell him anything. For the record, I went off on both before I left. The Douglas contract is my last contact with him. I'll make sure he gets whatever commission he wants, and that's it. After this banquet, I'm on a plane to L.A. early Saturday morning."

Sasha hadn't noticed Tamar's face until she stopped talking. Tamar leaned her head back on the headrest and squeezed the steering wheel.

"Girl, you okay?"

"I'm cool. I don't know, though. I think that's messed up if Elaine is dating Wes. That's dishonoring our sister rules about dating friend's exes."

"Doesn't mean a thing to her. But he's not exactly an ex,

so maybe that's why. She told me at rehearsal that she was going after him."

Tamar's mouth dropped open. "Oh yeah?" Well, you should've told her to back off. Whether or not he was your man didn't matter. He clearly gave you all his attention at the rehearsal and wedding."

"It doesn't matter to me. Maybe she was trying to sell him some property."

"Right. The property in between her legs."

Sasha laughed out loud, and within seconds, they both fell out laughing. "Girl, you are crazy." She told Tamar.

Tamar was laughing so hard, she had to wipe away tears. "I hope you get Mama Edmond's medication."

"Honestly? If I don't, I'm okay. Mom is doing great on her new regimen."

"I'm glad to hear that. You know, if you don't want Wes buggin' you, stay with us. Xavier won't mind."

Sasha shook her head. "My hotel is close to the event and the airport."

Tamar frowned and started the car.

Sasha put a hand on Tamar's arm. "I'm good. But, thank you."

Her apprehension about being in Atlanta had officially skyrocketed. Tamar's introduction to Wesley was meant to be a business contact, and Sasha blamed herself for allowing it to go beyond business. Hopefully, she could do her presentation and return to L.A. without him contacting her.

"Girlfriend, I'm sorry. Knowing Wes, I don't think he's

gonna let you go easily. He has the impression your relationship with him is deeper than friendship."

"Dang it, girl, you should've told me!"

"Remember, I introduced him to you as a potential source for your mom's medication.

Not a date. The offer to stay at our place is still open."

"Don't worry about me. He's not a serial killer, right?"

Tamar jutted her chin. "Of course not. He just goes after what he wants and usually gets it."

Sasha wagged her finger at Tamar. "You owe me a favor for introducing me to that man."

"Hmmm, not to my knowledge," Tamar smirked. "Anyway, that was your choice to date him."

Sasha was having difficulty knowing when or how to move away from negative people in her life. Wesley was at the top of her list. Kindhearted man, but no different from the others she'd dated. And she still wasn't sure about Damien.

Tamar drove to the hotel and stopped in front. Two young men approached the car, opening both doors.

"Thanks, but I'm not staying. I'm dropping off my friend." Tamar closed her door and turned to Sasha, "Call me if you need anything."

Sasha waved and exited the car with her carry-on. "I appreciate you. I'll call when I get to the airport."

"No, call me after the banquet when you get back to your room."

"Okay, Mama Hen. You sound like my Mom."

"I'm serious."

"Okay, okay," Sasha said before strolling into the hotel. She stalled at the door and looked around the hotel. A man in a beige coat was staring; paranoia overwhelmed her. She shook her head. This is ridiculous. Wesley had no idea where she was. She hadn't even told Dr. Douglas or Jonah. Out of all the hotels in Atlanta, how would he find her? She walked to the front desk and checked in.

Chapter 27

A bellhop assisted Sasha to her room. She thanked him with a tip and locked the door before picking up the remote to flip through the TV channels. Nothing seemed to settle her nervous energy. Tamar's words replayed in her head. *That's not his impression. He thinks you're his woman.* Not one time had she told Wesley they were dating exclusively. Maybe she should have refused the dates, and his help with the Douglas contracts and her mom's medication. She could have sealed that contract on her own. Maybe not the whole package, but at least one.

Her cell phone rang drawing her out of her wandering thoughts. *Damien.*

"Hello."

"Hey, sweet lady. What you doing?"

She smiled. "Talking to you."

"Right. Are you gonna be home this weekend?"

"I have an early flight back to L.A. on Saturday morning. I'm in Atlanta."

Sasha put in her Bluetooth and sat up in the bed. "Did you hear me?"

"I heard you. So, what's in Atlanta?"

"Work. I wish I didn't have to be here, but I'm here."

Well, I miss you and was hoping to see you this weekend. I have something to tell you, but I guess that won't happen this go round."

"I'm sorry. I guess we'll have to wait a bit longer."

"When?"

Sasha heard the irritation rise in Damien's voice; she ran a hand through her thick hair. "I can't say right now."

"I'll let you go, Sasha. I take it your answer to my question is it's over."

Her heart leaped at his words. "No, wait. Slow down. Don't put words in my mouth. He seemed impatient and angry, not himself. She didn't want to end their conversation with him upset.

"Every time I call, you either don't want to talk, or you blow me off. Like now."

"Damien, we've talked. You know how much I've been through, and this is not you. Patience has always been your strongest trait."

"Let's not forget I've been through stuff, too. Waiting, unsure of where our relationship stands."

"I said I love you."

"That's not what I'm talking about. Look, enough of all this. Whenever I see you again, we talk, or I'm outta your life. Good night."

He ended the call, and Sasha flopped onto her back. A single tear trickled down her face.

Chapter 28

The weather shifted from a sunny seventy-five degrees to low thirties that evening which called for a wardrobe change in her planned attire. Atlanta skies had dropped a snowfall two weeks prior, and this evening's chill in the air brought on a somber mood as light showers drizzled over Georgia. Sasha sorted through the extra clothing that she'd hung in the closet, her eyes settled on a black pantsuit. *This is perfect.* She hung it on the door and headed to the bathroom to shower and get ready.

After applying the finishing touches to her makeup, Sasha tucked her arms in a red coat and examined the red and black blouse that matched her black pantsuit. She added a red and black scarf around her neck to accessorize and turned her face from side-to-side. From her ruby red lips to her curly pinned up hair that flowed around her face, everything appeared in check. She picked up her briefcase and clutch purse, delaying her walk to the lobby.

She was not in a hurry to arrive at the banquet. Hopefully, Wesley had other plans and would not appear at the event tonight.

She received a notification on her phone that her Uber driver was arriving and rushed to meet him. The hotel where the physician's banquet was being held was less than ten minutes away. She entered the lobby, taking note of her surroundings. No Wesley. But she did locate the room where the event would take place.

"Ms. Edmonds," Dr. Douglas said, walking in her direction with a wine glass in his hand. "Thank you for coming."

"You're welcome. I have an early flight tomorrow and may not stay for the full event."

He sipped his wine. "Well, I hope you'll change your mind, but I do understand. Can I offer you some hors d'oeuvres or a drink? I'd like to introduce you to the other doctors."

Sasha followed Dr. Douglas across the room to a large table, greeting a plethora of his colleagues with handshakes and smiles. Although it was a part of her job, socializing with doctors and their spouses at this banquet was not what she had in mind when she'd agreed to attend. Her preference was to sponsor lunches, do her talks with the doctors and nurse practitioners and leave. But in this business, it was important to sell and find more sales on an ongoing basis. When Jonah Junior walked in, her tension gradually decreased. He walked over to Sasha and sat next to her.

"Hi, it's nice to see you again, Sasha. You look great," he said, hugging her.

"Thanks, Jonah. It's a pleasure to be here."

Jonah proved to be a pleasant distraction during the meal, and Sasha enjoyed chatting with him. Fifteen minutes before dinner ended, he escorted Sasha to an area where she could prepare for her presentation. He helped her lay out pamphlets about the company's products and free pens, pads, and penlights bearing Wexel Pharmaceuticals name and contact information.

Jonah stepped back and inspected the display. "These are eye catchers. It's a good thing they're free." He and Sasha shared a laugh. "I've be meaning to call and apologize about the meeting," he offered.

Sasha tilted her head.

"You know? At the hotel when I didn't show up."

She shrugged. "Oh, that. Your dad handled it. I'm sure he mentioned we got off to a rough start. I was surprised when he called for another appointment."

Jonah tugged at his shirt collar. "I heard. I had a talk with him, and he agreed to sign contracts for all four practices. Truthfully, he was quite impressed with you."

"I see." Sasha wished Wesley would show up here so she could tell him about his lying tail. Huh. She was incensed with him for taking all the credit for closing the deal on the Douglas contracts. If he had anything to do with those contracts, it was after she'd laid the groundwork.

Dr. Douglas walked in. "Almost ready?"

"I sure am," Sasha said, laying out another handful of ballpoint pens.

Dr. Douglas turned and left. Jonah watched his father stroll across the room. "My dad's not a bad guy. Like most doctors, he keeps his practice under control." He faced Sasha. "Well, go out there and win new clients."

"I'll do my best and thanks for your help, Jonah."

He smiled and gave her a quick hug. "Good luck."

Butterfly flutters in her stomach right before presentations were not unusual. She approached the podium and opened a bottle water, which normally alleviated her anxiety. Her major concern revolved around possibly seeing Wesley in the audience. He'd pulled off another big lie, leading her to believe he'd secured the Douglas contracts when all along, it was her efforts that closed the deal. But that didn't surprise her.

She opened her PowerPoint and briefly searched the audience before she started. The presentation would last approximately thirty-minutes, plus an additional ten minutes for questions. As each minute then second sailed by, the peace of knowing she'd get through without a distraction was evident. *It was finally over.*

Chapter 29

At the end of her presentation, Jonah Junior offered to take her to the hotel if she stayed for the entire event. When they arrived, Sasha exited his car and briskly walked into the hotel and up to her room. The minute she removed her key card and walked into the dark room, an eerie feeling caused a shudder. She'd left a lamp light on before departing. After flipping the light switch, she jumped when she saw Wesley sitting in the corner with a wine glass in his hand.

Sasha frowned. "Wesley. Who let you in here? How did you find me?"

"Tsk, tsk. I have my ways," He waved a finger. "What? No hug? No kiss? Darling, you're flunking Wesley's woman exam." He pushed himself up from the chair, summoning her with his hands as though she were a puppy. "Come here."

"I want you to leave. Now." Sasha demanded.

"I'm not going anywhere. I said come here."

His gruff tone made her tremble. Reluctant, but too fearful to say no, she went to him, using every ounce of energy she could muster to slowly shuffle in his direction.

Don't show your fear and you'll be okay. She paused a few feet away.

"Wesley, leave, or I'm calling security. You're obviously intoxicated."

He rushed toward her, pulling her into his arms, drenching her face and neck with wet, sloppy kisses. She could hardly breathe. She tried to push him away, but he tightened his hold.

"Stop!"

He paid her no mind.

"I said stop!" Sasha broke away, wiping her face of the alcohol stench. *Disgusting.*

"I've missed you. Why are you denying me the pleasure of your kisses?" His eyes devoured every inch of her body.

"Listen to me. This is all a misunderstanding. I'm not your woman, and... I mean we barely know each other."

His dark eyes popped out to the size of golf balls. The rage on his face was frightening. Sasha backed away, searching for answers to the one question she'd asked herself numerous times. How exactly did she think this would work? She was bright and should have seen right through his sweetie-pie, goody-two-shoes act.

"Our time together meant nothing to you?"

"Wesley, we shared a few meals as friends. We discussed my recent breakup with Damien. I never promised you a relationship. You knew where I stood." At this stage, it was a toss-up on how this conversation would end. Either the alcohol would enhance his false perception of their relationship, or this man's sickness would prevail.

Nonetheless, he didn't appear to be hearing or absorbing her words.

"Yeah, I took a hit from that idiot thinking we had something special going on."

"Wesley, I know you're upset. Go get some sleep. We can pick up where we left off when you're sober."

"I'm not going anywhere. I've had a few drinks, but I'm not drunk. Besides, you're leaving tomorrow. You think I don't know this?"

Wesley ambled across the room with a slight stagger. Through bloodshot eyes, he raked over Sasha's body, and she knew it was time to leave. She edged closer to the door then took off running. Her hand grasped the knob. He slammed the door shut and punched the wall.

"Don't. Run. Listen!" He pressed his index finger in her chest after every word. "Every day, I woke up with you on my mind. Waiting to hear from you. Your calls and texts stopped, and you stopped answering my calls and texts. You know how that made me feel?"

"Please listen."

"Listen to what?" He folded his arms across his chest. "You must think I'm nuts. Like that...that idiot Damien. You just used me to get your mother's meds. Or thought you could. And that punk Jonah. Yeah, I saw him hug you at the banquet. Then you left with him. What are you using him for?"

Sasha shook her head. "I don't use people. Jonah gave me a ride back to my hotel. He was being nice, and what did you do? Follow us?"

"You'll never know."

Tears welled in Sasha's eyes. She struggled to hold them back, catching the first tear with a finger. She looked at Wesley, trying to figure out how to escape. His eyes were more soulless than a dead owl's. His frown receded like the waves of the Pacific Ocean pulling away from the Hawaiian shore. She had no words left for this angry man hovering over her. Wesley portrayed himself as a real charmer in the beginning. In the end, he was condescending and irrational. Pleading with him to let her go was useless.

He studied her body from head-to-toe before he started unbuttoning her blouse.

"What are you doing?" She slapped his hand away.

"I'm about to show you how a real man makes love."

"Oh, no you won't. I'm not one of your office sluts." She frowned and started fastening the few buttons he'd unbuttoned.

Focused on buttoning her blouse, Sasha never saw the blow coming, but she felt it. His hand whacked her face so hard she heard her neck pop. He pointed his finger in her face. "Don't you ever talk to me in that tone again."

Stunned, her mouth wouldn't move fast enough to release the words she wanted to say.

"Did you hear me?" He shouted.

She pressed her left palm against her face and slapped him with her right. "Yes, I heard you."

She could see he was shocked that she had reciprocated. Not knowing what to expect next, she took a stance with her fists up, ready to swing if he attempted to hit her again.

Wesley's eyes narrowed. "Aha! You're one of those fighters. Good, because I've got something for you."

"I'm not violent, but you hit me first." She was too fearful to even twitch, but she wouldn't let him know it.

"That's the first time I've hit a woman. Make sure it's my last," he said coldly. "Now, take off your clothes and get in bed. I'd much rather tap that fine behind of yours."

With one hand on her hip and one in her jacket pocket, Sasha lifted her head to view the face befitting of the devil's. "No, hit me again and it'll be the last time you hit a woman."

"You gotta be joking." He threw his head back and let out a loud belly laugh. Within seconds, he quieted. His dark side resurfacing with a penetrating scowl. "You think you're so smart, but I've got news for you."

"That works both ways. I'm filing charges against you. Keep that in mind if you plan on hurting me."

"You wouldn't press charges against me."

"Oh, but I would. Try me. You never intended to help my mom or me. Why did you mislead me?"

He grinned broadly, his cold eyes bored into hers. "Mislead you? I helped you. And now I see how selfish you are." He rolled up his sleeves and said, "I'll tell you what. I may visit Victory in Peace Ministries and announce to the whole congregation what the bishop's daughter did. Somehow, I don't think dating two...well, Jonah makes three men at the same time is Christian-like." He waited for her answer. "Oh. You don't have anything to say now?"

Sasha's right eye twitched as she ground her teeth

together. *This guy is nuts.* She tried to hold it together, show her strength and not relent to Wesley's forces.

"Or even better. What if I call Camp Pendleton and tell Damien how much I enjoyed my tumble in the sack with you. And in case you're curious, we're having sex before I leave."

Still standing in the same place, she folded her arms. "Not while I'm alive. The thought of having sex with you disgusts me. You're despicable."

"Oh, I see. You're the kind of woman that forces black men to dilute the stock. Then you'll be the first to complain about us dating outside our race."

"That's ridiculous. You don't know anything about me."

"Well, prove me wrong. Marry me before Christmas, I'll cancel my plans for contacting your family."

She forced back a gag. "Not in a zillion years, you're sick."

Wesley walked closer to her and swiped her face with his hand. "Let's see if you think I'm sick after I make love to you. Do you like it fast and hard or long and slow?" He looped the scarf around her neck into a lasso and snatched her forward. Face inches from his, her lips quivered. "We have all night, I can mix it up too. Now, do as I say. Go lay down and take off your—"

Sasha sprayed his face with the pepper spray she'd retrieved from her jacket pocket. Grateful to that little small voice within who suggested she carry the spray in her pocket this evening instead of her purse where she usually kept it for emergencies.

Wesley let go of the scarf and rubbed at his eyes.

"Ahhhhh. Ahhhh. My eyes are burning! Call the paramedics, I can't see! Look what you did to me, you stupid bit—"

Sasha closed her ears to his nasty insults and swung the door open, fleeing down the hall. Sweat glistened on her forehead and face. Her heart was pummeling so hard, she thought it would break through her chest. Her only priority was getting to the lobby. Fast.

Huffing out breaths, she pounded the elevator button and waited for what seemed like forever. She glanced down the hallway a few times to make sure Wesley had not left the room. One minute, two minutes, three minutes passed. Where was the elevator? No man had ever hit her or said such vulgar things to her. If Wesley caught up with her who knows what he'd do next. She hit the elevator button again, nervously waiting for it to arrive.

A man's loud groans and mumbles echoed in the hallway. "Help me. I can't see!" Wesley. Holding towels against his eyes, stumbling around, feeling walls and doors to find help, he maneuvered closer. She gasped and kicked off her heels, running to the stairwell. She was on the tenth floor, but it didn't matter. She had to escape. Sasha ran down the stairs and kept running as fast as she could until she reached the first floor. She bolted through the door to the lobby undeterred by the long line at the concierge's desk.

"Excuse me," she said, making her way to the front. "I need help. A man was in my room when I got back. I pepper-sprayed him, and he could use some medical attention."

"Where is he?" the clerk asked, picking up the phone.

"Near room 1302."

With trembling hands, Sasha pulled several tissues from a Kleenex box on the manager's desk. She wiped her face and sniffled as she tried to respond to his questions. Her primary concern was who let Wesley in her room. Whoever was responsible should be reprimanded and suspended or fired. A male employee knocked on the door.

"Yes," the manager asked.

"Ms. Edmonds' friends are here," the employee said, slightly opening the door.

"Are you expecting friends?" The manager asked Sasha.

"Tamar and Xavier?"

"Yes, Ma'am." He opened the door for them.

Tamar entered first, and Xavier followed on her heels holding a drink carrier with drinks. "You okay," Tamar asked, touching Sasha's arm.

"I'm better, a little shaken up."

"Honey, the green tea is Sasha's," Tamar said.

Xavier handed Sasha the cup of tea and offered her some sugar packets and a stirrer.

"Any idea how Wesley accessed your room," Xavier asked Sasha while watching the manager.

"None. All I know is he was in my room when I returned. Somebody gave him a key or opened the door." Her mind was jumbled with a gamut of emotions. "I'm sorry. This is Mr. Jassett, the General Manager. He's investigating."

"Hello, Mr. Jassett. I'm Xavier Evans, and this is my wife,

Tamar. Could you tell us what you know about this situation?"

"Evans?" Mr. Jassett picked up his glasses and put them back on. "Wait, are you with that big law firm Evans, Porter, and Wilson?"

"I am, but I'm not here in an official capacity. We're here to support our friend."

Sasha stirred her tea and gave Tamar a 'here we go again' look. After Xavier promoted to partner two years ago, Sasha had shared with Tamar that she noticed a shift in his attitude. She said his ego inflated to the size of a hot air balloon, and you couldn't tell him that he wasn't the sharpest big wheel in Atlanta, flashing his business card at parties and social events. Tamar had disagreed and chalked it up to Sasha not being around him much.

"He's not my lawyer," Sasha reiterated. "They're both good friends."

The proclamation didn't seem to matter. Xavier still cross-examined the man about what happened as if he were on trial. The manager said they presently had no knowledge of how Wesley obtained access to the room and insinuated Sasha must have opened the door. Security informed them that after Wesley received medical attention, he told them he and Sasha had been dating, and she let him inside.

Sasha appreciated her friends' support. She found Xavier helpful in asking pertinent questions and assisting her with retrieving necessary information she required from a legal standpoint. In her frame of mind, there was no way she would have thought of the appropriate questions to ask the general manager.

Xavier, being Wesley's friend, convinced Sasha to cancel a call to the police, warning her of the negative media coverage and legal problems it would create for Wesley and ultimately his family-owned pharmaceutical company. Initially, Sasha was firm in her stance to file a police report, but she pondered the number of potential damage others might suffer from the fallout and didn't have the heart to hurt anyone else because of Wesley's stupid behavior. She did plan to file a restraining order to prevent a reoccurrence of tonight's event and demanded Xavier warn Wesley that she would follow through with pressing charges if he didn't agree to stay away from her family and Damien.

Two security officers escorted Sasha and her friends up to her room to collect her items. The general manager offered to switch her to a luxury suite with one free night, but Tamar and Xavier insisted she leave with them. They would take her to their place for the night and ensure she arrived at the airport safely the next morning. After such a hellish evening, Sasha was grateful for friends who cared.

Chapter 30

By the time Sasha reached her car, her father had left a voicemail instructing her to meet him at The Serving Spoon Restaurant. His voice sounded off-key and barely audible rather than robust and articulate. Sasha hoped her mom was okay. Nothing, not even a grouchy member–and there were many–could shipwreck the proud bishop's life except his precious first lady's health issues.

Sasha drove into the parking lot of her father's favorite breakfast spot and parked next to his car. She smiled when she caught him waving from inside the restaurant.

"Welcome to The Serving Spoon," the hostess said.

"Thank you, my dad has a table for us."

"Oh, okay. The waitress will bring your menus."

Sasha walked to the table where her father stood with open arms.

"You made it, huh?" He hugged her.

"Yes, and this time my flight was fine," Sasha laughed.

"I'm glad to hear that."

"Good morning," the waitress said, handing them menus.

My name's Mandi, and I'll be your server. You need a few minutes?"

"Yes, please. Kitten, do you want coffee or tea?"

"Sure, I'll take a cup of tea. But I'm ordering. Give me the turkey bacon, eggs scrambled well, and grits. No bread."

"I'll have coffee with pancakes and sausage."

"All righty, be back shortly." The waitress collected the menus and walked off.

"How's mom?"

"Have you noticed your mother's health is improving? She's getting out more and back to working in her garden some days. Praise God."

Her dad's face shined brighter than a row of floodlights. She smiled. "Wow, that's awesome news, Dad. And now that you mention it, she has seemed more spry than usual. Her new medication must be working."

"So far, yes. And her blood pressure has been lower."

The waitress brought their drinks and set them on the table. Her dad's expression shifted to one of concern.

"Okay, if it's not Mom, what's wrong?"

He poured cream and sugar into his coffee. "Two issues, but first things first. What I have to say is not easy."

"Well, what is it?" Sasha felt herself growing jittery. "Please don't tell me you're sick."

"No, nothing like that."

She took a sip of tea and breathed in courage. Maybe it was just another dissatisfied member threatening to leave the church or somebody else complaining about a problem in the church that wasn't a real problem.

"Tell you what, let's eat first, then we'll talk."

"Dad, come on."

"Kitten, trust me on this one. I don't want to spoil our appetites." His eyes held a plea.

The waitress returned with steaming hot food, and the scent made Sasha's stomach grumble. They held hands as Sasha blessed the food. She was determined to enjoy this father-daughter time.

A half-hour later, Sasha wiped her mouth and pushed her plate aside. "Okay, I'm ready."

Her father rubbed his hands together. "I have another daughter," he said in a near-whisper.

"What do you mean?" She frowned.

"It's true. I had an affair and fathered a child outside my marriage. But that was a long time ago, and for years..." He sighed deeply. "I had no idea she existed. Made the biggest mistake of my life trying to help her mom. I, well... Before I knew it, I got too involved. She never told me she was pregnant, just left the church."

"Does Mom know?"

He shook his head. "How could she? I didn't know until Shavon contacted me several months ago. I had to know for sure. A DNA test confirmed me as her father."

"You got the DNA results. But you didn't tell mom?" She searched her father's blank face. Sasha couldn't remember ever seeing him look so distraught. She wondered if he was wrestling with the negative way this longtime secret might alter his life. There were so many questions she wanted to ask but couldn't. How would it change what he'd done or the fact that her mother didn't know?

"The minute I got the call..." He folded his hands and stared down at his coffee. "I should've told Odette. But I hadn't taken the DNA test yet. With her health issues, I didn't want to upset her."

"But you knew she had to know."

"Yes, and I've told myself the same thing every day. I realized later how selfish I was. I went through a restoration period, praying for God's forgiveness. The Lord knows how much I love your mom. I denied the affair back then because I didn't want to hurt her, and I wanted to keep my family together."

Sasha drew in another deep breath and readjusted the wrap around her neck. "So, what are your plans?"

"We'll talk Sunday evening after we get home."

"That's likely the best time." Sasha watched her father fumble with his hands and stir his coffee. His discomfort was apparent. "And when do I get to meet...? What's her name?"

"Shavon and I'm not sure. Let me get through this ordeal with your mother first. Oh, Ebony asked me to remind you of the meeting after church tomorrow."

"Tomorrow? Oh, the WIP meeting. It slipped my mind. She's introducing a couple of new members."

They discussed a few church-related issues, and while they were talking, the fact that her father was not without fault crossed her mind. The man of God her mom adored and the members respected and followed, had at one point let everybody down in the worst way. He'd made a mistake when he was younger and committed infidelity. Yes, he'd made his peace, and still with all the prayer and repentance, one stone rolled onto his pathway. Sasha had no words, she just hoped this stone would not ruin her parents' marriage. At this point. Nothing else mattered except her mother's reaction after her dad talked to her about his other daughter.

Chapter 31

Rainy weather had ruined Sasha's plans to treat her parents to Sunday dinner at Lawry's Steakhouse. Lawry's was the restaurant her parents favored for special occasions like their anniversary, birthdays, or Mother's Day. Indeed, today was not a particular day, but Sasha made the reservation thinking a filet mignon or New York Steak may mitigate some of the gloom that overshadowed her father's somber mood. Then her father called to say they had considered takeout on the way home. He wanted to get her mother out of the lousy weather to decrease her chances of catching a cold.

Sasha opened her blinds and watched the wind hurl leaves across the lawn. Raindrops trickled down the large picture window in the living room, and the downpour had not let up in over an hour. Dad was right about the rain. Maybe she'd text him about stopping by the house after they picked up dinner. He hadn't asked her to be present when he told her mother about Shavon, but she knew her father.

Shocked at the time on the wall clock, she placed her plate in the dishwasher and jogged to the room to dress.

Where had the time gone? Late was not in her vocabulary, but she was slightly behind and needed to leave for church.

Thoughts of Damien not calling came to mind as she set the house alarm and exited. He'd said he wanted to talk and would be in town this weekend, and she was a little concerned that she hadn't heard from him. Though the weather may have forced a change of plans, which was understandable, his usual practice included a call. Her commute was slowed by heavy traffic, but she finally pulled into a reserved space in the church parking lot and grabbed her umbrella from the back seat.

After entering the sanctuary, one of the ushers guided her to the front row pews, but Sasha stopped at the middle aisle since services had started. She hadn't been to church in weeks and hoped to remain incognito.

A quick glimpse over the sanctuary revealed a steady flow of members drifting in. That was a good sign. Her father enjoyed preaching to a full house. He said a full house kept him motivated to win souls.

Her eyes roamed to the front of the church and stopped on a man who looked like... That's Damien. *Why is he sitting so close to the front? How strange.* He hadn't called to say he was in town. Oh well, she sighed, deciding she really didn't care while an inner voice reminded her that she did.

Memories of her father's earlier congregation in comparison to the one now was astonishing. She observed additional members filling the sanctuary. Over the years, the great Bishop Edmonds' sermons had spawned thousands of members, and his congregation continued to grow. She watched her father approach the pulpit wearing a scant grin, a purple robe, his minister's chain and cross. Only she knew the amount of pride he'd lost and the extent of pain he'd endured. He kneeled demonstratively for prayer and then took his seat in the pastor's chair with ministers on each side. Across from the ministers' section was his first lady draped in splendor, appearing regal in a black and white suit and hat to match.

Sasha's smile faded when she thought about what would take place between her parents this afternoon. After praise and worship, the choir performed several songs, announcements were read, and her dad stepped to the podium where he placed his bible.

"Good morning, saints! It's wonderful to see so many of you here at service today. Rain or sunshine, we're here to serve the Lord. Praise God. My sermon today is entitled, A God of Promise." He put on his glasses. "Our scripture comes from Genesis 32:24, King James Version. 'And Jacob was left alone: and there wrestled a man with him, until the breaking of the day.'"

"Amen," the congregation said.

Her dad preached with an animated stage presence and, boy did he preach. She'd heard him preach thousands of sermons, but this sermon. Something about the way he delivered this sermon drew her in on a deeper level than expected. Sasha couldn't take her eyes off her father as he paced the platform, leaping in the air like a whirlybird then dropping to his knees. He had the whole congregation on their feet throughout most of the service.

Catching a three-second breath, he leaned into the mic and lifted his hands. "So, my faithful servants of God, I say to you on this day. Life is tough, but do not become dismayed. Remember the scripture and Jacob's struggles. Along your journey, you'll have mountains to climb, rocky roads, and deep seas to cross. You may find yourself wrestling with life's issues as Jacob did but think of Jacob's history of wrongdoing in his past. It was God's promise that enabled Jacob to change."

"Glory to God," members shouted and danced in the aisles, praising God.

Her dad removed his glasses and placed them on the stand. He pointed to the congregation. "You, you, and all of you! Be assured that if you walk with the Lord and seek His divine guidance in all that you do, if you trust in His Holy name and wait on Him, He will never fail you. He will break that chain of bondage. He will carry you through the desert, storms, and floods. Psalm 145, verse 13 says, 'The Lord always keeps His promises; He is gracious in all that He does.' Believe it and receive it. And when you do, don't forget to have a forgiving heart. I've had members tell me, oh, Sister so and so... I don't speak to her anymore."

The congregation let out a hearty laugh.

"But can you really be a Christian and not forgive your friends, family, co-workers, and others?"

Sasha thought about what her dad said. Had she forgiven Damien? Elaine? Did this mean she should forgive Wesley for assaulting her? And what about Amy, Dayle, and Mike at Wexel? Was her heart a forgiving heart? She didn't know

God's plans for her or exactly how she was supposed to walk these things out, but she said a silent prayer asking Him to open her eyes and her heart to receive His guidance and do His will.

At the end of his sermon, Bishop called for those in need of prayer. One-by-one, members flocked to the altar, some in tears, others shouting praises. She saw Damien rise and walk to the altar. *What is he doing?* He kneeled, seemingly overwhelmed with emotion. The last to rise to his feet, Damien remained at the altar even after the call for membership was made, and the new members were led out of the sanctuary. *What is going on?*

Bishop called Damien to the podium and put his hand on his shoulder.

"I'm sure you've all seen this young man around the church. This is Damien Taylor, and he's been helping with the children's ministry for months. I want to announce that because of his services, we'll be able to offer our teens table tennis lessons this summer, and that's a positive move. It'll keep our youth off the streets and close to the church."

As members applauded, a collective, "Amen," rang through the congregation.

"Not only has he won championship table tennis matches, but he also has another talent. This young man is a head chef in the military. If you can't cook, we have good news. If you can cook, we still have good news. This is for men and women."

The congregation laughed and applauded as several 'amens' bellowed across the sanctuary.

"Damien's going to be teaching our church how to cook healthy meals. Several members of our community have health issues and seeing your doctor, changing your diet, and exercise are crucial parts of healthy living. Praise God. So, we're thankful for Damien, but that's not all. For those who don't remember, we had the privilege of him joining our church last month." He looked at Damien. "Uh, I'll let you tell the rest."

"Thank you, Bishop," Damien said as he stepped to the mic. He looked over the sanctuary, his gaze landed on Sasha. "Uh..." He chewed his bottom lip then inhaled a deep breath. "I'm so honored and blessed to be here. Pray for me 'cause I'm a little nervous," he said with a chuckle.

"Take your time, young brother," a male member shouted.

Befuddled by his behavior, Sasha caught every quirk she'd never seen in Damien. Nervous? He was hardly ever at a loss for words. And why was he in the pulpit?

"I've been through some things, and they made me realize I wasn't living right. So, I started asking for forgiveness. I asked God to work on me, and He did. Working here with Bishop reminded me of my call to ministry. At first, I said no; I'm not worthy." He shook his head. "But I also said, Lord, guide me. I've been preaching in the military, sometimes to the incarcerated population, but He said it's time to do more."

Someone in the congregation shouted, "Amen. That's all right."

"Then," Damien sucked in a breath and exhaled, "when

the call came again, I talked to Bishop and prayed, 'Lord, guide me.' This fall, I've committed to finishing what I started a few years ago, my Master's in Theology. Thank you, and God bless you." Damien moved to the side, and her father embraced him.

"We serve a mighty God. Let's congratulate Damien again," her dad said, extending his arm toward Damien.

Sasha arose as everyone stood and applauded.

Shortly after the congregation's applause and cheers, Bishop announced, "And by the way, while he's in seminary, he'll be on our staff of ministers."

Damien glanced at Sasha. Eyes staring deep into his, she tilted her head and blinked. Theology School? Ministry? Teaching cooking lessons at the church? He couldn't be serious. What about his dreams of owning his own restaurant? She noticed he shifted his eyes to her dad. Within a few minutes, she'd figured it all out. This decision likely came under the tutelage of none other than Bishop Martin Edmonds, who had tenderly planted the seed of ministry into Damien's brain.

Chapter 32

Following the benediction, the congregation filed out in clusters. Sasha searched the crowd expecting Damien to come find her. She spotted him in the opposite aisle bolting to the exit door, and before she could reach him, someone tapped her shoulder.

"Sister Edmonds let's go have lunch. I need your opinion on something."

Keeping her eyes on Damien, Sasha said, "Thanks, but I can't today. Call me, and we'll get together soon."

Brief greetings with members who wanted to chat as she maneuvered through the crowd delayed her departure. By the time she left the sanctuary, she was running to catch Damien. She noticed him racing to the parking lot. *Why was he in such a hurry?* She wanted to chat with him. The light turned red before she could cross the street, halting her progress. When the light changed, she dashed for the parking lot as fast as her feet could carry her. After she neared his Jeep, she waved both arms.

"Damien!" *Did he hear me?*

He got inside his Jeep and backed up.

"Damien!" Out of breath, she banged her palm on his passenger side window.

He let the window down. "Hey, you tryin' to get run over? I didn't see you."

"I'm sorry. I tried to get your attention. But you jetted off so fast, I asked myself, why's he rushing?"

He cut the engine off and unlocked the doors. "Climb in. If you have time," Damien said with a sarcastic tone.

She opened the door and slid onto the passenger seat, immediately sensing a difference in his mood. Gone was the usual cheery, full of jokes disposition that she knew. His serious attitude left her with immense discomfort. She faced him.

"How's everything going?"

He kept his focus straight ahead. "I'm blessed."

"I thought you'd call me when you got here. And what's up with the seminary?"

"Tried to call, but you stay busy. I figured you'd find out about school sooner or later."

"I'm not that busy," she clasped her hands. "I mean, we chat on the phone quite a bit."

"We used to. Not so much lately, and last time you cut me off."

"I understand. Either I was out of town or leaving. You know how busy my schedule is.

"Being busy is not new for you," he said after an extended period of silence.

Bothered by his nonchalant tone and attitude, Sasha felt uncomfortable viewing the lateral part of his face. *Why won't he look at me?* "What made you do this? You're a phenomenal chef with so much to offer. And what about the restaurant you wanted, and playing table tennis?"

"I have goals, too. The restaurant's coming in time." He rested his hands on the steering wheel. Right now, my main purpose is the ministry. I started seminary school and dropped out, but never had a chance to tell you."

She crossed her legs and said, "Don't go there. You had opportunities to lay everything on the table. Obviously, you didn't want me to know about seminary."

"Can you blame me? It's not like you would've cared."

"That's not true. I care about you, and I wouldn't ask if I didn't care." She arched her brow. "Tell the truth. My father is the reason behind this, right? It's not like he can hand the church over to me."

For the first time since she entered the car, he turned and faced her with a blank stare. "I make my own decisions, okay? Yeah, working with Bishop inspired me, but don't think I'ma stop cooking or playing tennis. That's a part of who I am."

"Sure. Teaching cooking lessons and tennis at the church, though?"

"What's wrong with teaching at the church?"

Sasha leaned forward. "I know you. You have a competitive nature, and professional cooking and tennis are your passions. Look at all the trophies you've won. And you're giving up all those treasures for the ministry?"

"Listen, I'm not worried about treasures. The bible says,

'Lay not up for yourselves treasures upon earth.' I recommitted my life to Christ."

Folding her arms, Sasha blew out a sigh. "Well, I'm confused. Not too long ago, we made love. Hot and spicy, down-to-earth love in my shower. Without being married. Now suddenly you want to be a minister?"

"Yeah, we made love many times. And my rationalizing that it was okay because we were engaged was wrong. It wasn't okay, and I've repented. Have you?"

Sasha glared at him. "I'm not answering that."

"You don't have to." Damien's head rested against the headrest. For a minute or two, he said nothing. "So much happened to me before that Georgia incident. My head wasn't on straight. When I got back..." He stopped in mid-sentence then stroked his hair. "You don't know half the story. Flying out of town to find you could've cost me my military career. Thank God, it all worked out."

"You had no business in Atlanta anyway."

"Listen, Georgia is my hometown, and my folks are there."

"Well, back to the ministry. Say what you want; I still believe my father pulled out all the bells and whistles to get you in the ministry and you fell for it. You can't do school, military, tennis, business—"

Damien chuckled. "You're wrong as two missing feet. Bishop's a good man, and he loves his family and the church. He led me back to the ministry, but the final decision was mine. I know God's got my back on this. You know," he pointed to her. "You're not an easy woman to love anymore, and I don't honestly think love is important to you."

"Why? Because I'm a bold, motivated woman and I refuse to be controlled and hoodwinked?"

He touched her cheek and smiled. "If you think that's the reason, you need to re-evaluate your life. It's all water under the bridge, though. I've made my peace." He checked his wristwatch. "Listen, I gotta go."

She stared at him, wondering what happened to the Damien she once knew. "Now that I can talk, you don't want to?"

"I have plans today."

The bitterness in his voice and the way he whisked his eyes over her before shifting his view was chilling. She searched for the appropriate words to say but could not think of any.

"Guess it's time for me to go. I still have the ring if you want it."

"Keep it for now. I'll get it."

She got out of the car feeling flustered and disappointed. She loved Damien with all of her being and had never intended to hurt him. A view of him replicating her father's behavior and committing infidelity was branded in her head. Her father would finally have the son he wanted, but not a shallow daughter who would walk behind her husband as a gesture of obeisance. She'd seen her mother become a shadow of a renowned minister, an antithesis of the educated school teacher she once was. That would never happen to her.

They had talked for over an hour, the conversation veered in many directions except the right one. And what about Monica? If he wasn't dating her before, was he dating her now? She wandered through the parking lot, wishing she could recant the words she'd said to Damien.

Darn! She had forgotten to join Ebony after church for the Women in Prosperity meeting. She had placed her phone on silent during church and forgot to turn it back on. As she walked to her car, she turned the ringer on and noticed Ebony's number was flagged urgent. She played the message.

"Sasha, call me now!" Ebony's voice sounded jittery. "Your mom got sick at a restaurant. Paramedics are taking her to Saint Francis Medical Center. Clutching her chest, she screamed "No, no, no-o-o!" She spotted her car and ran.

Chapter 33

Past frazzled, Sasha drove like she was on the Indianapolis Speedway. She flicked a tear from the corner of her eye and tried to focus on the road. What happened to Mom? Daddy said they were picking up food and going home. Did she get sick inside the restaurant? Was it food poisoning? Her heart? Had Daddy told her about Shavon?

All the unanswered questions raised her anxiety tenfold. Her cell phone rang once. Twice. Three. Four times within two minutes. Someone should've guessed by now that she was on her way to the hospital and couldn't answer. Bluetooth or no Bluetooth, she had to get to the hospital. She wasn't interested in hearing a preliminary report over the telephone; she needed to see, hear, and touch her mom to confirm that she was okay.

Traffic flowed smoothly until she reached the 105-East. At that point, it gradually slowed, then picked up again. She blew her horn and banged the steering wheel when a Corvette cut in front of her car. She slammed on brakes, almost rear-ending the driver. Sasha pressed her hand against her forehead and inhaled to stop the Ten-K marathon in her chest.

"Crazy driver!" She shouted, gripping the steering wheel tightly.

She swerved into the hospital parking lot and sprinted through the Emergency entrance to the front desk. Four windows were closed with one clerk on duty and five people in line. *Where the heck is their staff? This is the Emergency Department.* Sasha glanced around the full waiting room looking for her father. Her mind was spinning, a cauldron of emotions ready to make her scream.

"May I help you," the clerk asked.

"Yes. Is Odette Edmonds here yet?"

"Are you a relative?" The woman asked.

"Her daughter. My friend said paramedics were bringing my mother here."

"Give me a minute, and I'll check."

She watched her pick up the phone and dial.

"Oh, Lord, please let her be okay," Sasha mumbled under her breath, tapping her foot to alleviate the perpetual fear of losing her mother.

The clerk tapped on the window to get Sasha's attention. "I can't let you in yet. Please take a seat."

Sasha waved her hand. "I don't want to sit. Is my father back there?"

"Yes, Ma'am. I'm sorry, they won't allow any more people in. They're working on your mother."

"But I'm her daughter. I must see her. Please let me in."

"Tell you what, I'll recheck in fifteen minutes and update you."

That wasn't what she expected to hear. Sasha was close

to the edge. Didn't this woman understand fifteen minutes might be too late?

"Fifteen minutes? No, I can't—" A hand on her shoulder distracted her attention away from the clerk. Damien stood behind her.

"Let's step aside and talk," he held her arm, guiding her to a corner area.

"Is Mom okay? Please tell me she's alive."

His red eyes told a different story. "They think it's a ruptured appendix, and they're preparing her for surgery."

Sasha was unnerved. She couldn't ever remember a time when she'd seen Damien cry. "Ruptured appendix? Oh, no. What's her condition?"

Damien chewed his bottom lip. "Critical, but stable. I'm sorry."

She went blank and couldn't breathe, think, or even realize she was falling.

"Whoa!" Damien said, steadying her with a firm grip. "Let's sit down. She's awake." He helped her to a seating area away from other people.

What could have possibly happened? She'd seen her mom this morning at Sunday services, now they were about to rush her to the operating room barely clinging to life. Every worst-case scenario scrolled through her head.

"I need to see her or talk to the doctor. I'm concerned, surgery is serious."

Damien sat beside her and leaned close. "We got this. Okay? Like I said, Mom is awake and talking. She said not to worry about her. Me and Bishop spoke with the doctor, and your dad's not leaving her side until they roll her to O.R. We prayed before I walked out."

Sasha bowed her head and took a deep breath. "Thank you. I'm glad you're here." She asked Damien, "Do you mind giving me all the facts and please don't leave anything out?"

"The doctor," Damien paused, "said they would have to perform emergency surgery to remove your mom's appendix or she might die. He also said all surgeries have risks, but with your mother's health conditions, hers were higher."

It wasn't easy to listen to the information Damien shared, but she tried to focus. A vision of barging through the Emergency Room door like a heard of bulls clouded her mind. What if this was her last opportunity to hug her mom, tell her how much she loved and appreciated her? It perturbed her that they were preventing her from seeing her mother.

She watched Damien's face with an appreciation of the daunting task he had endured. Most people wouldn't have bothered, not after what occurred between them.

He placed his hand over hers and squeezed gently. "It's hard to say this," his voice cracked, and he blew out a long sigh. "The doc said Mom may not survive surgery."

Knowing the disclosure regarding her mother's surgery was difficult, she watched him grapple with his own state of mind while trying to support her. Sasha dropped her head, resting her face in her hands. "No, I can't take this," she cried. Damien covered her shoulders with his arms, providing consolation with gentle words. She leaned into his chest and wailed, no longer able to stifle the pain that burdened her. She heard him sniffling while he held her.

Time seemed to progress slowly during her mother's surgery. Every time she or Damien checked with the clerk, the waiting was made more daunting by a "still in surgery" response. Sasha paced the hallway near the small waiting area.

"Why hasn't Daddy come out to get us? He must know how worried we are."

"He will." Damien scrolled his cell. "Bishop didn't take the news about your mom very well. Before I left, he said he was gonna make some calls after they took your mom back."

Sasha saw her father walking down the hallway. He appeared to be searching for them.

She stepped into his line of sight. "Daddy, we're in here." Haggard, he walked into the small waiting area and pulled off his overcoat.

"How's Mom?" Sasha asked.

"She's out of surgery. I got to see her briefly before they rolled her to recovery. The doctor said he would be out to speak with us in fifteen or twenty minutes, so we need to go upstairs."

The bishop walked them up to the waiting room. Sasha sat next to her father, patting his thigh. She longed to reassure her father that she could support him through this crisis. She just needed to pull herself together first.

"That she made it through surgery is a good sign," Sasha said.

Her father took a deep breath. "Yes, bless her soul. That woman's a fighter."

"Bishop, can I get you some coffee or food?" Damien asked.

"No, but thank you. You know... I keep thinking, and the doctor said it's not so, but maybe I shouldn't have told her about Shavon. It might have caused a physical reaction. I... I feel responsible for what happened."

Sasha shifted her gaze to Damien and back to her father. "Dad, this is not the time."

"Damien knows," Her father said.

She folded her arms and studied her father's face. "Knows what?"

"About my affair and Shavon," her dad responded.

"Okay, that was your choice." Taken aback that he'd discussed his former mistress and daughter with Damien made her envious. For years, he'd concealed this information from his closest confidants in the church so him telling Damien came as a complete surprise. She knew Damien had built a close relationship with her parents, but she didn't realize her dad had allowed him to be privy to intimate family details.

"He's family now. This situation with your mom's health, Shavon... My spirit's drained, and there are times when the pastor needs prayer. It was time to reach out and not just to anybody. This young fellow held me up in there, and I thank you, Damien."

"Any time, Bishop. You know I got you covered. And like

the doctor said, Mama Edmonds' condition had nothing to do with you."

"Don't beat yourself up," Sasha said, touching her father's arm. "I'm sure Mom knows you love her." Her face softened as she hugged her father. What felt like an eternity passed before a weary-looking physician in green scrubs walked into the waiting area.

"Edmonds family?" The doctor announced, surveying the waiting room.

They walked over to the physician and formed a circle around him.

"I'm Dr. Patel. Mrs. Edmonds is in recovery. Her surgery was successful. She's stable, but because of the nature of her cardiac disease, we'll need to monitor her closely. She'll be in ICU a few days, maybe less if she progresses well.

"When can we see her?" Damien asked.

"She'll be a bit groggy when she's transferred. But after she's in ICU, check with the nurses."

Sasha and her father asked the physician several more questions. Before he left, he clarified their concerns.

"Listen, if you two want to grab a bite to eat, I'll stay here," her father said.

"It is about that time. What do you say?" Damien asked Sasha.

She shook her head. "I can't leave the hospital."

"We don't have to, the cafeteria is still open," Damien said. "You gotta have more than tea and coffee. And we can bring Bishop some food, too. Cool?"

She slid a glance at Damien, hesitating before she

answered. Heck yes, she wanted to eat with him. The hospital might not be the right time or place, but she had so much she wanted to say. If she didn't say it today, when?

"Sure," Sasha said picking up her purse. "You're absolutely right."

Chapter 34

The cafeteria was quiet but created a pleasant ambience for a private dinner. She and Damien walked past the food dishes. Damien selected a tuna sandwich and garden salad, and Sasha chose a chef salad for herself and beef stroganoff for her dad.

They sat at a table near the window. Damien spread his napkin across his lap and reached for her hand to bless the food. She studied him; picked up on the change in his behavior from earlier.

"What've you been up to?" He asked, pouring salad dressing over his salad before diving in with a fork.

"Work. That's changing, though."

"How so?"

She picked at her salad. "I'm resigning."

"What, resigning from Wexel? Why?"

"For one, to help mom recuperate."

"No, you know Bishop's not gonna let you do that. He knows you love your job."

Unable to eat more than a few bites of her salad, she placed her fork on the plate. "I did at one time. Wexel pretty much consumed my life, but no more. There are other priorities, and they require attention." She clasped her hands. "I'm sorry about the curve balls I threw at you. I was wrong."

"Curve balls? More like basketballs. But, hey...apology accepted, and I forgive you. You looking for another job?"

"Not right now; it's best for me to relax for a few months. I was passed up for the promotion. I can help my mother, and then when I'm ready, finding a job shouldn't be a problem." She stared upward. *Why is it hard to say something so simple?* "I, uh...I need to tell you something."

"Shoot," he said, biting into his sandwich. "Hey, you're not eating?"

"How can I eat? I can't eat. Can't sleep. Can't focus," she gave a wry laugh.

Brows furrowed, he leaned forward, giving her his full attention. "That's crazy. What's bothering you to the point that you can't eat or sleep?"

"You." She pushed her hand against her face. "Well, not exactly. What I'm trying to say is I'm in love with you."

"What?"

"Damien, I've never stopped loving you, and lately I've been thinking about how foolish I've been. I was too stubborn to admit it."

"You could've fooled me. What about the dude in Georgia?"

She forced her eyes to meet his. "The dude in Georgia was a business associate. He was full of crap. I cut all ties to him. I mean, he took me to dinner a couple of times. Made promises he couldn't keep. Like getting Mom into a clinical trial and on some new medication. All lies."

With his eyes on the salad, he asked, "If he'd gotten the medication. Then what?"

"He didn't. So, how can I honestly answer that question?"

"I can't be sure, but apparently he got your attention. You two went out more than once. Did you sleep with him?"

"Oh my gosh. Seriously, did you ask me if I was sleeping around?"

He pushed his plate aside, and a half smile slid across his face. "I'm sorry, but I have to know. I'm not trying to demean you, but I went through a lot of pain over you."

Sasha gazed downward. Mention of his pain hit hard, and she didn't know how to approach that topic. He'd stepped into forbidden territory. *How could he even fathom the idea of her sleeping with another man?* Sure, Wesley had kissed her, but that was it. If she could start over she would bypass the risks she'd taken that ruined her relationship with Damien. *Lord, if she could only change the past.*

"I guess we're even, then," she shrugged her shoulders. "Truthfully, I went out with him to increase my chances of getting medication for Mom. I thought you knew me. I can't imagine why you'd think I cheated on you."

"Because you thought I was cheating with Monica. And I wasn't. So, I guess we are even. You caught us being a little too friendly, and yes, I was wrong. But, I never slept with her." He took a sip from a bottle of juice. "Sasha, look. Let's not dwell on the past. I'm a changed man. I was lying in bed one night and the Lord revealed some points I hadn't considered. We both set ourselves up for temptation. We're both guilty."

"I see what you mean. We're human, Damien. Humans make mistakes." She waited for a reply, but he didn't respond. "Well, where do we go from here?"

"Let me ask you this. You say you love me. Why'd you wait until I nearly broke my neck to get you back before telling me this?"

She shrugged. "I wish I had a golden answer. Pride, stubbornness, thinking you had somebody else, not wanting to marry someone like my dad. All the above and more. Listen, I need to change, and I'll try my best. I'm asking for another chance."

He folded his arms across his chest and sighed. "In less than a year or so, I'll be an ordained minister. You said you don't want to marry someone like your father. Bishop is an awesome man of God, and I hope to follow his steps. My wife will proudly stand by my side and support whatever I do. And, together we'll head a ministry someday, and *children* is a must."

Her eyes found his. From the expression on his face, he didn't like what she had said. "I was speaking of my dad's infidelities. I've been hurt before. Betrayed by men. I'm constantly afraid of being made a fool by someone who claims to love me." She ran her hands up and down her arms. "I need to know that I'm enough. Call that selfish or whatever, but you're asking me to commit to everything you want," she said, exasperated. "You plan on having a church, too?"

"Maybe. I mean, I'll be part of a church and preach. Not run my own, at least not right away. My interest is prison ministry, a population not everybody wants to help. We'll see where God leads me. Bishop's been talking with me about taking his position for a while. He plans to tell the congregation about his daughter."

"How can he do that? The assistant pastor left, the other pastors are new. You're not a pastor; how can you take his job?"

"Only for a while. I'm not ordained, but I have experience. He may wait until I'm ordained and then leave or step down temporarily."

"What about us? Did anything I say make sense?" She touched his hand, and he placed his hand on top of hers.

"I'm being straight with you, Sasha. I'm a work in progress, and you'll really need to work on you. We'll talk some more. See if we can get it right this time."

She nodded. "I understand."

This man was everything to her, and how she'd managed to believe anybody else could match his qualities was a disgrace. If he decided not to take her back, she'd accept his decision. In the meantime, she would do everything possible to win his heart again.

When they returned, her mother had been assigned a bed in ICU, and they walked to the unit. Sasha and her dad went in to see her mom. She batted her eyes, watching them until she drifted off. According to the nurses, there were signs of improvement, but her status remained critical but stable.

At close to midnight, they left her father in ICU, and she

and Damien walked to the parking lot. Sasha was tired, but relieved that her mom was resting and stabilized. The night air was chilly, and she wrapped a wool scarf around her neck to stay warm while disarming the car alarm.

"You've been such a blessing to my parents and to me. I can't thank you enough," Sasha told him.

"Like your dad said, I'm family. Maybe not in a biological way or through marriage, but I'm church family. Your parents are good people."

"They are. Don't feel compelled to drive to San Diego if you're tired. You can have the other room."

"Nope, I'll pick up coffee and hit the road. Staying at your house is too much temptation."

"Well, just because it's temptation doesn't mean anything will happen, brother. But I get it."

He smiled, and they both laughed simultaneously.

"Ring me when you're back in town," Sasha said.

"I will. You'll see me in church."

Sasha entered the car and closed the door. Her eyes trailed Damien to his truck, wondering about his thoughts, goals, and if they included her. Everybody deserved a second chance. While praying silently, she hoped he wouldn't hold it against her that she hadn't given him one. Or decide that he wouldn't reciprocate her unforgiveness. Oh, how the tables had turned.

Chapter 35

Sasha slowly peeled off her spandex clothing piece by piece as well as a sweatshirt she'd put on at the hospital and headed for the shower. She toweled off and sprawled across her fluffy bedspread. Face turned up to the ceiling, she closed her eyes and prayed for a way out of the mess she'd created with Damien. He tried to be nice, but clearly, his thoughts were not leaning toward taking her back, and marriage was beyond her expectation at this point. Maybe she should move to the east coast after she quit her job. Several well-established college friends in D.C. and New York had approached her numerous times about possible sales positions. She could build a new life there and start over. But that would take her too far away from her parents. How could she leave them at a time when they needed her most? There was no way. Besides, moving anywhere out-of-state meant the end of her and Damien's relationship forever, and she was serious about winning her man back.

"Lord, please help me." She rolled over, curled into a fetal position, and prayed — over her mother's health, her father's challenges, and the potential loss of the one man who had truly loved her.

After tossing and turning for hours, Sasha prayed for blissful sleep. Just as she started to doze, the clamor of metal caused her to hop out of bed. The sound had come from the balcony. She grabbed one of Damien's tennis rackets from the closet and cautiously ambled through the townhouse, looking around. Her fingers rolled the mini-blinds open a tidbit so she could peek outside. She blew out a reedy breath. The stray cat who usually slept on the porch had knocked over the pan of food she'd left out.

Unable to sleep, Sasha walked to the kitchen and put on the kettle. Some chamomile tea would help relax her tense muscles, though she didn't think it would relax her mind. She sat at the kitchen table, dipping her tea bag in water and pondering on whether to call Tamar. A glance at the wall clock told her it was three fifty-three a.m., almost seven a.m. in Atlanta. Since their Spelman days, she and Tamar understood sisterhood meant being available at any time, and a quick girl's talk was necessary. She dialed Tamar's number.

"What can I say?" Sasha told Tamar. "You and Dad were right. I should've been five steps ahead on this one."

"Five steps? I'd say twenty to prevent another woman from hookin' him. And Bishop announced he's in the ministry? Girlfriend, you better wrap Damien up fast before the church sisters go after him."

She squeezed a lemon slice in her tea and added honey. "It won't be easy, and I blame myself."

"Don't kick yourself too hard. Any woman would've gone off if she'd seen her man with another woman. Y'all talked, now work it out. And forget about Dr. Jekyll and Mr. Hyde."

"Wesley is the last person on my mind, but you called it right. He has issues." Sasha pressed her fingers against her forehead, still wondering why she had chosen to overlook Wesley's negative behavior. All the signs had been there.

"I'm sorry for being so blunt. Me and Xavier got into it last night, so I'm a little pissed."

"No big deal. I'm sure newlywed spats are normal. Since when did you start apologizing for saying what's on your mind?" Sasha carried her tea to the bedroom and climbed into bed. She settled against the headboard. "My question is do you think Damien will ever trust me again?" Share your advice on how to get him back."

"Advice? You might not like my advice."

"Tell me anyway."

"Prove that you love him. Pray and go after your man. That's all I can say." She heard a beep on the phone. "Call me later. This is a client," Tamar said.

Sasha trudged into Wexel with a punctured mood. She was ready for a match with her bosses and would not bit her tongue about what's on her mind. She'd sent Dayle and Mike an email requesting an appointment to discuss Amy's job proposal and said nothing more. They were likely expecting her to take the position, and she didn't want them to conjure up a new proposal to persuade her to stay.

The most positive information to lift her spirit in weeks was her father's call about her mom's condition improving.

Her doctor had written orders to move her mom to a Step-Down Unit. Sasha navigated a hallway filled with multiple boxes of paperwork while thinking about her parents. It was too quiet in here. Silence in the partially empty office was unusual, and the environment heightened discomfort.

Promptly at 8:00, Dayle called Sasha and asked her to report to Mike's office. She removed the resignation letter from her printer and reread it multiple times before signing it. When she reached Mike's office, the door was slightly ajar. She knocked and walked in. Much to her surprise, Amy was there.

"Have a seat, Sasha. How was your trip?" Mike asked.

"It went quite well. Dr. Douglas was pleased."

"That's good to hear. We're hoping you've decided to work with Amy."

Sasha handed Mike the letter. "I'm sorry. I can't. Here's my resignation letter, and effective two weeks from today, I am leaving."

"May I ask why you're turning down this opportunity?" Amy inquired.

"Don't get me wrong. Wexel is a great company. I'm doing this strictly for personal reasons."

"We hate to lose you," Dayle said. "You're a terrific employee, and you work so hard."

"We don't have to lose her," Amy butted in. "What if I offer you a higher salary to take the position?" She rifled through the paperwork on her lap. "Here it is. I see you grossed one fifty last year with base pay and commissions." She flipped through the paperwork and scanned it closely.

"My initial offer was one seventy-five annually. What about one-ninety and any commissions earned if you want to keep several clients?"

"This has nothing to do with money. At first, my disappointment was over not being selected for the regional director position. But the job or the money is no longer important for me."

"Well, what do you want?" Mike asked, tapping his pen on the desk.

"Can I please interrupt for a moment?" Amy moved to the edge of her chair and faced Sasha. "Sasha, you're our top sales executive for the L.A. and Atlanta offices. We laid off four sales executives last week due to reduced productivity. I didn't want to do it, but I had to. Any sales rep here would jump at the opportunity I'm offering you. Plus, in a year, you'd take over my position when I leave for Europe. And, the sky is the limit on bonuses and benefits based on productivity. You sure you don't want to reconsider? Maybe think this over and get back to us in two or three days?"

Sasha's gaze traveled to Mike, Dayle, and back to Amy. She smiled. "I'm sure. If you had made this offer a month ago, I probably would have said yes. But now, my mindset is different, my priorities are different, and they're more valuable than what you're offering me. Thank you, but my resignation is final. I'll make sure my accounts are up to date before I leave."

Sasha exited the room, feeling like the weight of Mount Everest had lifted from her shoulders.

Chapter 36

Free at last. She was glad that her meeting was stress-free and non-toxic. Now that she had resigned from Wexel, she'd focus on spreading faith seeds and flourishing in church and her personal life.

"Will six o'clock be okay for the ladies?" Sasha checked in with Ebony about the WIP ministry meeting.

"I think so. Most are home from school or work by then. I called everybody last night and left messages."

"I really appreciate your help, Ebony. I hope everyone can make it."

"No problem, girl. I'm getting ready to feed little Miss Asia. I'll see you later tonight."

Sasha ended the call and scrolled through her text messages. Excitement she had not felt in a long-time lifted her spirit. Damien had texted her. *Hello, Sweet Lady, hope your week is going well. Good to hear Mom is progressing well. That's a blessing. Talk to you soon. Love, Damien.* She covered her mouth. *Sweet Lady?* He hadn't called her Sweet Lady in a while. Maybe he would take her back. Sasha didn't want to get her hopes up, but she prayed he would see her efforts to change and become a better person. She closed her eyes and took a few deep breaths.

####

Sasha's stomach gurgled. This is becoming a problem. Maybe it will settle down before the meeting. She drove into the church parking lot and counted the number of cars present. She hoped most of the ladies showed up tonight. She wanted to announce what she'd planned to tell them on Sunday before she left the church to catch up with Damien. She opened her purse and searched for an antacid. She popped two in her mouth and chewed, confident they would alleviate the churning in her stomach. She walked into the Crystal Room, and Asia ran to greet her.

"Auntie Sasha!"

"Hi, honey." She stretched her arms to receive Asia's hug and kissed her cheek, touching the little girl's medium length braids. "Don't you look pretty in that cute dress?"

"Mommy made it," she said, spinning around to show off her dress.

From a distance, Ebony, who was chatting with a couple of the members, waved and headed in her direction.

"Glad you're here. Not everyone could make it. Lanice couldn't get a babysitter, Madelyn's ride didn't show up, and I don't know what happened to the others." She blew out a winded sigh.

Sasha hugged Ebony. "Take it easy. It's all good. We'll make another announcement on Sunday."

Ebony nodded her head, looking around the room. "Okay. Well, there's twenty-four of us here. The other new member confirmed, but she's not here yet. And Asia's here 'cause my cousin forgot she was babysitting."

"Asia can stay." Sasha squeezed Ebony's hand. "This was last minute, and I didn't expect everybody to come."

Sasha walked toward the front and took her place behind the podium. "Good evening, beautiful Women in Prosperity! Thank you all for coming out. Let's open with prayer. Sister Juanita, do you mind?"

Sister Juanita walked to the front and led the group in prayer. After the prayer, Sasha looked at the women who'd joined the ministry she'd started to help shape ladies into prosperous women.

"First, I want to thank Sister Ebony for filling in for me when I was absent. Second, I want to apologize for my absences, and I assure you I will be here to lead you from this day forward. I want all of you to know how proud I am of each one of you. You came in here with different struggles and obstacles to overcome, and some are still facing various problems, be it single-parenting, financial struggles, unemployment, relationship issues, finding a babysitter—" Some of the ladies laughed. "—or just struggles in believing in your own potential. But," she held up her hands, "if you stay focused and keep God first, nothing is impossible."

Ebony bobbed her head to show approval of Sasha's words.

"Even though I'm your leader, I haven't been a positive role model. I've sinned by making poor choices, and I've hurt people, some of the closest people to me who loved me dearly." She paused and glanced at Ebony who pressed her hand against her heart as a sign of encouragement. "I fell short of God's glory. But what's great about God is that He forgives, and He's not as concerned with you or me falling, He wants us to get back up and push forward." Sasha fought back tears and kept a smile on her face. She used a moment of applause to wipe her eyes.

"You see, keeping God first and staying focused on your goals are critical components of truly being a prosperous woman. There was a time in my life when I thought..." She took a deep breath and blinked back more tears. "There was a time in my life when I thought being a prosperous woman meant excelling in my career, having everything I needed, no matter the cost to others. I had an "*I*" mentality." She stuck a finger to her chest. "*I* need this, *I* need that. And that selfishness got me nowhere."

She cleared her throat and let her gaze fall across the women in the room. "So, I stand here today ministering to you ladies and to remind you," she pointed at them. "It's not about how far or fast you can climb the ladder of success in life, and God knows it's not about how many heads you have to step on to get there. An "*I*" mentality will make you lose focus on your true goals. And when you lose focus, you'll find yourself on a dead-end street wondering how in the world did I end up here?"

"Amen," several women shouted.

"So, let's love God first, love yourself, love your family, and love on each other. We come here to serve the Lord, and to provide service to our church. Stay prayerful and faithful, and I'm here if you need me."

The women gave Sasha a standing ovation.

She held up her hands and laughed. "Thank you, and now that I've got that sermonette out the way, I want to talk about our upcoming Spring Gala Fashion Show. Sister Ebony is going to present her fashion designs, and we need volunteer models, including Asia, to participate."

Cheers, applause, and amens filled the room. Sasha was glad to see the ladies were willing to step in and help Ebony prosper.

"What kinda clothes are we gonna be modeling?" A young woman asked.

"Can we choose our outfits?" Someone else asked.

"Slow down. These are questions Ebony will address. She's the designer, and you'll wear whatever she designs for you. I'll have more information at the next meeting. For now, please be sure to sign up on the list if you're interested." Sasha waved the sheet in the air.

Smiling at Ebony, she said, "See, I told you I would handle it."

Ebony waved her hand, and she and Sasha touched palms. She held up her cell and played back Sasha's testimony.

Sasha's face glowed. "Girl, you were taping me? I didn't comb my hair, add more lipstick or nothing."

"You look fine, and your testimony was powerful." Ebony tapped her phone. "There, I sent it to your cell and email."

"Thank you."

A young woman sitting in the back row waved. It was Roxanne. Sasha hadn't noticed her earlier. *How long has she been here? Is she stalking me? How did she find me?* Sasha tried to rein in her thoughts. She was sure there was some plausible reason for Roxanne showing up here.

Ebony waved back. "Oh, she made it. That's our other new member, Shavon. Let me introduce you." Ebony started walking toward Shavon.

"I'll be there in a minute." Sasha leaned against the podium. She held her stomach and inhaled a cleansing breath. Roxanne was Shavon? The grumbling in her stomach continued, and it bustled like the roar of a thick tidal wave. *This can't be real.*

Chapter 37

The fire blazing in Sasha's stomach and a combination of nausea was ruining the end of the best WIP meeting she'd ever had.

She ran to the restroom to regain composure and take another antacid. She plopped down in a chair and guzzled some water. Heightened curiosity, along with a sense of uncertainty, made her feel ambivalent about Roxanne. Why was she here and what was her purpose for joining the WIP ministry? Sasha didn't blame her for wanting a relationship with her father, if he was her father. He must be. How many Shavons had she met in her life?

As the other women started filing out of the Crystal Room, Sasha walked back in and observed Roxanne talking to Ebony.

"Hey, I was looking for you," Ebony gestured for her. "This is one of our new members. Shavon, this is Sister Edmonds, our pastor's daughter. You'll meet the other new member at our next meeting."

Sasha extended her hand to Roxanne. "Welcome, you'll have to excuse me. I'm a little on edge with this upset stomach." The expression on Roxanne's face was difficult to discern. Ebony was family, but it wasn't the right time to break the news about Roxanne.

Roxanne accepted her handshake. "Thank you, I'm sorry about your stomach. I loved your testimony."

"It was long overdue. I'm glad you had a chance to hear it. We'll talk before you leave."

Roxanne nodded and quickly looked away, fumbling with her braids. Sasha shot her a few side-views, attempting to analyze and predict what was in her head. *She knows full well what they'd talk about. Like why is she here? Money? Blackmail? Something else? Roxanne, Shavon...whatever her name is, will know up front, that won't happen.*

Voices in the hallway caught everyone's attention. It was Bishop, and the other voice sounded like Damien's. Sasha tilted her head. I thought he was at the base.

"I think that's a good plan, then we can—" Bishop paused after he and Damien entered the room. "Sorry, I... I, uh, forgot about your meeting," Bishop said, smoothing his hair back. "I guess you two met each other?" he asked Sasha.

"We're getting acquainted," Sasha said, looking at her father.

"Hi Bishop, Damien. I gotta drop off a member, she's in the car with Asia," Ebony said.

"Drive safely," Bishop said to Ebony.

Sasha hugged Ebony. "I'll call you this week."

"Okay. We'll talk later."

Sasha's attention shifted to Damien. "When did you get back?"

He hugged her. "I never left. I'm heading out in the morning."

"Damien, this is Shavon, my other daughter. Damien is one of our ministers in training."

"Nice to meet you," Shavon said, shaking Damien's hand.

"Ladies, can we meet in my office? Let me have a word with Damien, and I'll be right there.

"Shavon, can you stay?" Sasha asked, picking up her purse. Shavon nodded yes and followed Sasha down the hallway to the office. Sasha was not ready for this. Who would dream of getting through the most terrifying flight ever and then later discover your sister was sitting next to you? A sister. Someone she knew nothing about until her father told her.

They entered the office and sat in front of a cherry wood mahogany desk. In silence, Sasha observed Roxanne checking out the desk, cabinets, and décor. Sasha crossed her legs and scrolled through her texts and Facebook page, wondering why Damien had stayed as opposed to returning to the base. The door opened, and Bishop strolled in.

"Let me say this, I apologize for not introducing you earlier," Bishop said.

"Dad, we know each other. I met her on the plane," Sasha answered.

"When?" He asked, putting his glasses on.

"Remember the hairy flight I told you and mom about? The new intern at Wexel?" She gave Roxanne a side glance. "We were on that flight from Atlanta together. And then she called my company to get an internship with me. I know her as Roxanne."

"I called Wexel to inquire about an internship program and mentioned your name. I promise that's all, and friends and family call me by my middle name. Shavon," Roxanne explained.

"Use of two names can be deceiving." Sasha's tone was icy. "Did you know who I was when we met?" She removed a bottled water from her purse and sipped. This was not the attitude she should have, but she had to sweep away the debris in case Roxanne had an agenda. Protecting her father and his image was important, and she wanted to make sure this reunion would not bring unexpected problems, like someone trying to blackmail her father.

"Honestly, I didn't. I came to the church a few months ago and again recently. In church, your name was mentioned, and I checked your business card. Only then did I put it together.

"My plan was to introduce you two, not have you meet like this." The bishop pressed his hands together. "Shavon, my wife knows about you, and we'll invite you over. My burden is the congregation doesn't know." He released a long sigh. "I've prayed and asked the Lord to give me answers on how to proceed. I'm certain He will."

"My struggles are what brought me here but..." She pulled her braids back, "I won't join the church or WIP if it'll hurt your ministry. From what you've told me, this church and your family are important to you."

"I can't deny you membership. Our church doors are open to everyone," Bishop said.

"Do you have a church home?" Sasha asked, still feeling uncertain about Roxanne.

"No, I left my other church." She gazed at the floor. "After a while, I didn't feel comfortable there."

"If you have no church home, you're welcome to join our church. WIP has an awesome group of women, and they're a great support system," Sasha said.

"In time, I will tell the congregation about my past," Bishop told Shavon. "I have to determine when."

Sasha turned to Roxanne. "And, I'm not sure if Human Resources told you, but I put in my resignation at Wexel."

"They did. The internship program was put on hold."

Sasha shook her head. "I'm sorry. I may have some friends that can train you. Call me next week."

"I will and thank you."

The meeting went on, and Roxanne shared her story, which particularly touched Sasha. She learned Roxanne had been abandoned by her mother when she was six years-old. She was placed in foster care, moved from home-to-home until a family adopted her at age nine. Closure of a lifelong desire to connect with her family drove Roxanne to research her family roots which led her to Bishop. Sasha now understood why meeting her father was important to her. She could not imagine growing up without parents to guide and support her. As she listened to her sister speak, empathy and love filled her heart for this hurting young woman.

Sasha stared at Roxanne. This was her sister. It didn't matter how she got here, she was blood, and Sasha would try to build a relationship with her, personally and through ministry.

"That's my story," Roxanne said, looking down. "Thank you for listening."

"You're welcome. We're family now." Sasha touched the girl's arm before turning to her father. "I have something to share too, Dad. Ebony recorded this tonight." She handed him her phone and pressed play on the video.

Smiling, his face brightened as he watched Sasha's testimony. "Amen, amen! Can I send this to the ministers? I'd like this video shown in the WIP announcement on Sunday."

"Sure. I believe Ebony had that in mind, too."

The Bishop handed Sasha her phone. "I'm glad we had this time together. Let me give my daughters a hug for their strength and for giving me strength."

He opened his arms and together, Sasha and Shavon walked into their father's embrace.

Chapter 38

Sasha's cell signaled a text message. *Can I still stop by before I leave? Please text me when you get home. Love, Damien.*

She walked into her townhouse, dropped her purse and laptop on the couch and sprinted to the bedroom. She'd told Damien he could stop by and she wanted to freshen up. What could he possibly want to talk about at this hour? She changed into a cute pink t-shirt with "Blessed and Highly Favored" on the front and a pair of black stretch pants. Thankful that her upset stomach had subsided, she turned on the kettle. Why was she so nervous? Was he officially ending their relationship?

She walked back to her room and picked up the blue velvet box that held her engagement ring.

"Please, Lord, don't let him ask me for this ring back," She prayed, clutching the box to her chest. A multitude of negative thoughts streamed through her head — him saying, "I have a new girlfriend," or "I don't love you anymore." She cringed and closed her eyes, unwilling to accept the ridiculous thoughts. The doorbell rang, and her heart started fluttering. She had almost reached the front door before she realized she still held the velvet box in her hand. She quickly placed it inside a blue vase on the coffee table, ran her hands through her hair and went to open the door.

"Hey."

Hey? *Was that all he had to say?*

"You made it." She stepped back so he could enter.

He removed his coat and walked over to the fireplace, rubbing his hands together. "It's kind of cold outside."

"Yes, the weather this year is different. It should be getting warmer by now. I'm making tea. You want some?"

"Nah, I'm cool," he said, following her to the kitchen. "I saw something tonight, and it brought me to my knees."

She put the red tea kettle she was holding back on the stove and walked to the kitchen table where he sat. "Wow, what did you see?" She pulled out a chair and sat next to him.

"Remember, what we talked about? You, me. Works in progress?"

"I do."

"I have to admit. I had doubts about us getting back together. My ministry, the way my life is going in a different direction... Bishop sent me a video of your testimony, and it blew me away."

Sasha slapped her forehead. "My father sent you the video? I tell you...that man."

"It's okay, though. Your testimony kept me from making a mistake. I love you, and I want to marry you."

"Yes, Yes!" The tips of her fingers pressed against his face, and she gently kissed his lips. "Oh, babe! I love you, too.

Wait." She ran to the living room and removed the velvet box from the vase.

"You're ready for a repeat proposal, huh?" Damien laughed.

"No, I wasn't. I mean, yes, I am! But that's not what I was expecting. I thought maybe you were going to ask for the ring back," she handed him the box, "not put it on my finger again."

He pinched her cheek and smiled. "God had other plans." He removed the ring from the box and bowed on one knee. "I love you way too much to give you up, Sasha Edmonds. Will you be my wife?"

"I sure will," she said, bending her hand down. He returned the ring to her finger, pulled her close and kissed her passionately. She broke away, fanning her face. "Uh, we better stop." They both laughed.

"Right," Damien said. "No hanky-panky until we're man and wife."

Chapter 39

Nine months later – Victory in Peace Ministries

Sasha hardly believed this day would come, and she was ecstatic. In less than two hours, the ceremony would begin, and she would finally become Mrs. Damien Taylor. Glancing around the room at her friends, Tamar, Lynne, Carleen, Ebony, Elaine, and her sister Shavon, she felt blessed. A bigger blessing was reuniting with Elaine after their estranged relationship. Frequent reminders to herself regarding forgiveness, made Sasha reconnect and ask Elaine to be part of the wedding.

Glancing at the ladies, Sasha admired their custom designed cranberry gowns with short jackets and large multi-colored rhinestone necklaces and earrings to set them off. They were gorgeous, thanks to the creativity of Ms. Ebony.

Tamar waddled over and placed her hands on Sasha's shoulders. "You ready for this, girlfriend?"

"I am. And what about you? Can you stand long enough for us to tie the knot?"

She rubbed her swollen belly and smiled. "Yep. If this

little girl or boy settles down. Been kicking me harder than a kickboxer."

"Girl, don't make me laugh."

"You laughing but wait until you get pregnant."

Sasha shrugged. "I'm up for it, and you know Damien is ready. We're waiting a year, then it's on."

"A year? Uh, huh." She gave Sasha the "I don't think so" look. "Don't place your bet on a year. We said two, then bam! Pregnant three months later."

"If it happens, it happens. We'll be in our new home by then." They touched palms in agreement.

"Hey, ladies. You okay?" Sasha asked the bridesmaids who were engrossed in chatter.

"Yes," they all said at the same time.

"What time you gettin' dressed?" Ebony asked Sasha. "That wedding planner, um...what's her name?"

"Amiya," Sasha said, checking her manicure and adding lotion to her hands.

"Oh, yeah. Miss Prissy Amiya will be here soon." Ebony bent her wrist and rolled her eyes to the ceiling.

"All right now. Don't criticize my wedding planner. She's... Well, she's somewhat different. But, I'll say this, the woman's no-nonsense, and she knows her stuff."

Ebony pursed her lips. "If you say so." She opened the closet and moved a few robes around. "Where's your gown?"

"It's in there."

"I don't see it."

"What?" Sasha hopped to her feet and raced to the closet.

She looked inside a black clothes bag that was nestled in the corner. "I thought for sure it was here." She opened the bag to find several of her dad's clergy robes. "Darn it! My Dad forgot to bring the gown. He was supposed to put it in here last night."

"Whoa! Girlfriend, you don't leave your wedding gown anywhere. Gowns come up stolen, you know," Tamar said.

"You're right, but the church is alarmed. Nobody broke in here." Sasha shook her head. "I meant to check the garment bag when I got here, but Amiya called and I forgot."

"Did I hear you say somebody stole your gown," Elaine asked.

The chatter among the ladies stopped; they lifted their heads and focused on Sasha.

"Stole your gown?" Carleen asked, frowning.

"Oh, wow! Who would do that?" Lynne asked.

"No, no. It's not stolen," Sasha said, raising her hand. "I'm sure it's in my dad's car. I hope, anyway."

"I should've kept the gown and brought it myself. You think he's at the house?" Ebony asked.

"I'm not sure. Let me call him because I don't know which car he's driving." She dialed her father's number, but he didn't answer. Her mom didn't answer her cell either. "Oh boy, looks like I'm getting married in my silk robe or sweat suit."

"We gotta get that gown," Ebony said. "I'll go see if Bishop's in his office."

"I'll check the sanctuary," Shavon said. "He might already be here."

"Okay," Sasha nodded. "And listen, if you run into anybody — sound tech, organist, security — tell them to have Bishop call me pronto!" She checked the wall clock and plopped down in a chair. Please show up soon, Dad.

Sasha had been stressed, the good kind of stress that all brides-to-be go through. She should have slowed down, but how? There was so much to do before the wedding, and some days she forgot to eat. She had lost a couple of pounds and didn't realize it until she tried on the gown and it sagged. A saggy gown on her wedding day? No way would that happen, and Ebony had saved the day with minor alterations. Before this day was over, she'd likely lose a few more pounds if she didn't find that gown before the wedding started.

"It'll be okay," Tamar said to Sasha.

Sasha nodded and dialed her dad's cell for the tenth time. A bride forgetting her gown was unusual, but she did get off track. It didn't matter, she'd walk down the aisle in anything, including the sweat suit she wore today. She was marrying the love of her life. She grinned, envisioning the look on Damien's face if she came down the aisle in a sweat suit.

The door opened and in walked Ebony and Shavon, carrying the missing gown. Everybody applauded.

"Woot, Woot!" Tamar said. "Back in business. Now our bride can get married."

"Thank you very much," Sasha said, as Ebony hung the dress on the closet door. She rolled her neck. "Uh... FYI, I was getting married. Today. Gown or no gown."

"I know that's right," Tamar said.

"Bishop's eyes got real wide when we rushed up to the car. He apologized and said he forgot the gown was in the car," Ebony said.

"My daddy, bless his heart."

"Let me help you get dressed," Ebony said, running her hand over the dress.

Amiya knocked once then barged into the room and gasped. "How come you all are not downstairs?" She pointed at her wristwatch. "The wedding starts in thirty-three minutes. And you," she said, wiggling her fingers at Sasha, "why aren't you dressed yet?"

"My father just got here with my gown," Sasha explained.

"What?" Amiya gave Sasha the craziest look. "Hurry up, please. I'm not used to operating on CP Time. And the parents just arrived with the ring bearer and flower girl. Everyone should be downstairs." Hands on her hips, she prattled on. "Ladies, line up at the sanctuary door in five minutes." She sprinted out the door faster than a racehorse on fire.

"Mmm, she better cut them energy drinks and coffee," Tamar said, rubbing her belly.

Comments floated around the dressing room about Amiya being hyper as the ladies primped their hair and touched up their makeup, snickering. Sasha was grateful for Amiya's madness, it added a dash of humor that she needed to calm her nerves. Ebony helped her step into her gown, the hairstylist and makeup artist came back to freshen her hair and makeup to flawless. After the hairstylist handed her a mirror, she felt like a princess who was marrying her prince. Her mother and Damien's mom entered, and they all left the room, giving Sasha and her mom a moment alone together.

A plethora of words sailed through her mind as she attempted to remain calm. Don't trip over your gown. Try not to cry and ruin your make up. Think positive images, and they'll come to light. Thank God for this day.

One-twenty. Ten minutes before the wedding party would march in. One of Amiya's assistants handed out the bouquets and escorted them to an area of the church where they would wait until Amiya called. Everyone lined up, Sasha and Bishop were last. The bishop's face shined as he examined Sasha from her veil, down to her white A-line, off the shoulder, ivory lace gown with beaded pearls.

"Kitten, you're gorgeous." He planted a light kiss on her forehead.

"You're looking spiffy yourself in that tuxedo."

He nodded. "I feel good. My daughter is finally getting married."

"All right," Amiya interrupted. "The music will start in five minutes."

Sasha closed her eyes and inhaled, shaking off her anxiety. The minute she heard Brian Courtney Wilson's song *A Great Work*, a sense of calmness was present, and the line began moving forward. She could feel her heart pumping, beat-by beat. One at a time, each couple marched forward until everyone had walked down the aisle except Sasha and her father. Everyone stood up as she entered on the arm of her father. It seemed like forever before she reached the altar and received the comfort of Damien's smile. He was fine in his black tuxedo, and he didn't take his eyes off her. Sasha glanced over at her mom who winked. Her mom wore a permanent smile that Sasha imagined would be stamped on her lips forever.

Her father gave her hand to Damien and walked to the podium to start the ceremony.

"Thank you, and God bless you all for being here to see Mr. Damien Taylor and Ms. Sasha Edmonds become man and wife. Amen."

The ceremony was just as Damien and Sasha had planned. Short, concise, and no extras, until the end. Bishop closed the ceremony with a prayer for Sasha and Damien then said, "I now pronounce you man and wife. Damien, you may kiss your bride."

Damien lifted Sasha's veil, wrapping his arms around her as their lips locked in a passionate kiss. The guests shouted and clapped. They broke the kiss and Damien grinned.

"Whew! I can do this now, y'all. This is my beautiful wife."

Face-to-face, they stared into each other's eyes and embraced once more. Sasha was Mrs. Damien Taylor, the happiest woman in the world. Relief washed over her as peace streamed in deeper than a quiet river.

Her dad said, "I present to you Pastor Damien Sean Taylor and First Lady Sasha Monique Taylor. May God bless their marriage and ministry."

Sasha and Damien joined hands, faced their guests and lifted their arms. Applause rang out as everyone cheered.

After the audience simmered down, Damien said, "Okay, just a short announcement about the music we chose for our wedding, and we'll head for the reception. Please join us, 'cause you know the food will be tasty."

A young woman got up and shouted something he couldn't understand. He put his hand to his ear. "I can't hear you."

Sasha whispered, "She asked about the reception location."

"You don't know where the reception is?" He frowned.

"The Snooty Fox Inn?" The young woman asked.

"No, baby girl. We won't be in South Central. Other end of town, Ritz Carlton – Marina del Rey. Somebody give her the address, please."

Sasha watched Damien and smiled. *He is such a gracious man.*

"Okay, you know we walked in to Brian Courtney Wilson's song *A Great Work.* Well, me and my wife struggled through parts of our relationship, but God led us back together after the storm. We pray the Lord will do a great work through us in ministry and our community. And we chose these inspirational songs that reflected encouragement and joy. Tasha Cobbs-Leonard's song, *This is the Freedom* reminded us of how God had blessed us to experience love, restoration, joy, and peace." He extended his hand to Sasha.

"We've stepped into the joy of the Lord. Ready, Mrs.

Taylor?" Sasha grasped his hand. "Please worship with us for a few minutes." Damien and Sasha bowed their heads. A spotlight shone on them. *This is the Freedom* started, and they sang along with the song.

"*Step into the Joy of the Lord. Step into the Joy of the Lord.*" They waved their hands and swayed back and forth, leading their guests in praise and worship. During parts of the song, they swung around to face each other and sang while holding hands. The bridal party sang and swayed along with them, and soon, all the guests were on their feet waving their hands and singing along. Waving and swaying, Damien and Sasha exited the sanctuary leading the way to Step into the Joy of the Lord, and the wedding party trailed two steps behind them.

About the Author

Reading and daily journal entries were the catalyst to Patricia's first novel, *Reflections of a Quiet Storm*, published by an independent publisher in 2009. An avid reader, her previous published work includes two books, multiple short stories, monthly health care columns for an online magazine, and several health care articles for a local newspaper. She also enjoys reading Women's Fiction and Romance novels, which occupy many seats on her bookshelves.

Patricia is a Family Nurse Practitioner and a Psychiatric-Mental Health Nurse Practitioner, she holds Adjunct Nursing Faculty positions at two universities. She is a member of the National Black Nurses Association/Council of Black Nurses – L.A., Sigma Theta Tau International Honor Society of Nursing, Black Nurses Rock, California Association of Nurse Practitioners, and International Black Writers & Artists. Patricia's church home is Greater Zion Church Family in Compton, CA. She considers music, reading, and prayer as the keys to relaxation and creativity, and she loves spending time with her family.

Patricia's short story appears in the Brown Girls Books Anthology *Single Mama Dating Drama*, an AALBC two-time Best-Selling book. *Two Steps Past the Altar* is her third and latest novel. She is currently working on her fourth novel.

Visit her online at http://www.patriciabridewell.com/

Made in the USA
Lexington, KY
17 July 2018